"Is this some kind of joke?"

Jan stammered as she asked the question.

"I don't joke about such matters. You asked to take your sister's place, and that is what you will do."

"No way!" Jan was on her feet, pulses racing, heart thudding against her ribs. "I'm leaving right now."

"You are not." He had risen with her, his black eyes like stone. "We have an agreement. You will fulfil it."

"You can't make me!" Her trembling hand clutching the back of the chair, was white-knuckled. "There's no court in the world that would uphold that paper I signed!"

"No court in England, perhaps," Don Felipe countered. "But this is Spain. My country."

KAY THORPE, an English author, has always been able to spin a good yarn. In fact, her teachers said she was the best storyteller in the school—particularly with excuses for being late! Kay then explored a few unsatisfactory career paths before giving rein to her imagination and hitting the jackpot with her first romance novel. After a roundabout route, she'd found her niche at last. The author is married with one son.

Books by Kay Thorpe

HARLEQUIN PRESENTS

853—SOUTH SEAS AFFAIR
902—DANGEROUS MOONLIGHT
941—WIN OR LOSE
973—JUNGLE ISLAND
1084—TIME OUT OF MIND
1141—LAND OF ILLUSION
1204—TOKYO TRYST
1261—SKIN DEEP

HARLEQUIN ROMANCE

2151—TIMBER BOSS
2232—THE WILDERNESS TRAIL
2234—FULL CIRCLE

KAY THORPE

steel tiger

Harlequin Books

**TORONTO • NEW YORK • LONDON
AMSTERDAM • PARIS • SYDNEY • HAMBURG
STOCKHOLM • ATHENS • TOKYO • MILAN**

Harlequin Presents first edition September 1990
ISBN 0-373-11301-3

Original hardcover edition published in 1989
by Mills & Boon Limited

CHAPTER ONE

As STUDIES went, this one had to be in a class of its own, Jan reflected bemusedly, gazing around the lofty room with its superbly moulded wall and ceiling panellings and heavily loaded bookshelves. The great central chandelier was supplemented by wrought-iron lamps, as yet unlit, of course, at this hour of the afternoon. Two huge leather sofas were placed facing each other on either side of the fireplace, while the desk near where she stood was almost monolithic in its carved solidity.

Don Felipe would be with her in a few moments, the manservant who had shown her here had said. She only hoped that the Spanish interpretation of a few moments coincided with hers. She wanted to get this initial interview over and done with.

Not that there could be any problem. Raine had already informed him of the substitution. A job in a million, she had called it. So far, Jan had seen nothing to dispute that assessment. Her first view of the *hacienda* itself had taken her breath. Pillared and porticoed in sparkling white stone, with the coastal mountains as a distant backdrop, it was straight out of the pictorial travel-books.

Working in a place such as this could only be a good move—especially when compared with the cramped office that had been her abode up until one short week ago. Gary had been loath to let her go, but he'd really had no choice in the matter.

How she could have allowed herself to become in any way involved with a man who was not only her employer, but married into the bargain, Jan still hated to think. Thank heaven she had come to her senses before the affair had reached the point of no return. Even if Raine hadn't come up with this opportunity, she would have had to leave the company. From now on she would steer clear of entanglements until she met someone who was free to return her feelings.

Turning to look out through the deep window embrasure, she saw a man crossing the inner courtyard. Taller than the average Spaniard, he was wearing riding breeches, and a white shirt which she judged to be silk from the way it sat on his lean frame. Crisply styled black hair surmounted a face which had an almost hawklike quality in its tautly boned angularity. In his early thirties, Raine had said. If that was Don Felipe himself, then this was going to be no sinecure of a job. He looked the kind of man who would command and expect instant compliance with his every whim.

So stop finding difficulties before they even arose, she chided herself as he passed out of view. This was another country, a whole new way of life. At least give it a chance. Personal secretary to Don Felipe de Rimados—wasn't that worth making a few adjustments for? Raine had to be well and truly overboard about the man she was going to marry to give up such an opportunity.

She made a swift appraisal of her reflection in the nearest of the gilt-framed mirrors, seeing a slender figure of medium height, dressed in a pale grey linen suit that had started the day pristine fresh, but was by now looking a little travel-weary. Not a lot she could do about that right now. Don Felipe was aware of how far she had come. He would no doubt make allowances.

Cut long at the back to slope up to the level of her ears at the front, her hair, at least, had withstood the rigours of plane, bus and taxi journeys. The stylist had wanted her to have the natural dark gold colour highlighted, but she had refused. A new job and hair-style were enough innovations to be going on with. Even her face looked quite different framed the way it was, blue eyes brilliant with mingled excitement and nervousness.

Behind her, the door opened. Steeling herself, Jan turned to meet the rapier-keen dark eyes of the man standing in the doorway. Black brows drew together as he studied her.

'Whoever you are,' he said coldly, 'you are not Miss Presley! What exactly are you doing here?'

His English was excellent, Jan noted fleetingly. It was her turn to frown. 'I don't understand,' she said. 'Raine contacted you to say I'd be taking her place. She——'

'I had no message.' There was steel in his voice, the well-shaped mouth thinned to a taut line. 'You're saying she isn't coming back?'

'I'm afraid not.' Jan felt as if her heart could sink no further. Raine had lied to her; she had to have lied! Why, she couldn't begin to imagine. 'I'm sorry,' she began haltingly, 'there seems to have been some mix-up. I was under the impression that my sister had gained approval from you for the replacement.'

'Your sister?' One eyebrow flicked upwards. 'You bear little resemblance.'

'Raine is my stepsister,' she explained. 'Her mother was married to my father. He adopted Raine legally. That's how we have the same surname.' Her shoulders lifted in a helpless gesture. 'I'm as taken aback as you obviously are, *señor*. So far as I knew, everything had been arranged.'

'I've had no contact with your stepsister since she returned to England almost two weeks ago,' he stated. 'She was to have just two more days before I began proceedings.'

'To recover the advance on salary you gave her, you mean?' Jan was doing her best to retain her poise. 'She passed that on to me, too. Naturally, the money will be returned if you decide I'm not suitable for the position.'

Don Felipe's eyes scanned her features, dropping to appraise the rest of her with the same almost clinical detachment. Jan forced herself to stay cool under his gaze.

'You're fully aware of the conditions governing the contract?' he asked on an odd note.

'Of course.' She had little idea of what conditions he might be talking about, but she had no intention of rocking the boat any further. Raine's reasons for dropping her into this situation might be obscure, but the job itself was still worth fighting for. 'I'm qualified on all counts,' she added. 'Including a good grasp of your language.'

'That would remain to be seen.' For the first time he revealed a simmering anger in the sudden set of his jaw. 'For what reason did your stepsister decide to renege on our agreement?'

She refused to allow herself to be intimidated by the clipped demand. 'She's getting married.'

'Married?' The anger gave way to some other emotion, less easily defined. 'To whom?'

A man, it was on the tip of her tongue to retort. She bit it back with an effort. 'Someone she's known quite a while, but she never expected him to ask her.'

'A love match?'

A faint warmth rose in Jan's cheeks at his tone. 'Is that so unlikely, *señor*? People fall in love all over the world.'

'And out again very quickly, for the majority.'

'That's a cynic's viewpoint,' she flashed, unable to quell the impulse. 'It's easy to see you've never been in love yourself!'

The strong mouth twisted. 'A rare perception,' he observed, 'if somewhat lacking in the finer points of diplomacy. It isn't my habits, emotional or otherwise, that we're discussing. Your sister signed a contract with me. I would be within my rights to demand satisfaction.'

'She's done her best to provide a substitute,' Jan pleaded. 'I'll do everything that's required of me. Just give me the chance to prove myself.'

Don Felipe had closed the door, and was standing with his back to the carved wood, eyes narrowed as he scrutinised her afresh. She had begun to lose hope when he finally spoke.

'I have to give the matter consideration. In the meantime, I'll have someone show you to your room.'

She stayed where she was as he moved towards the bell-rope by the fireplace. At least he wasn't turning her out right away. Her eyes assessed the powerful breadth of his shoulders as lifted an arm to tug at the rope, the narrowness of waist and hip. Not a handsome man in the accepted sense of the word, but one who positively reeked of pure masculinity. Hawklike had been the thought that crossed her mind on first sighting. Seen in profile as he turned, the strong jut of nose and firm jawline did nothing to destroy the impression. That mouth of his could be cruel, she judged, and she felt a sudden apprehensive quiver along her spine.

'Dinner will be served at nine o'clock,' he said. 'You will give me the pleasure of your company.'

'Shall you have your decision made by then?' she asked boldly, and saw the dark head incline.

'Perhaps. There is much to be taken into account.'

Jan failed to see why. The proof of the pudding, as they said, had to be in the eating. If he wasn't satisfied with her performance, he could always tell her to leave. She had spent none of the advance Raine had turned over to her so far, so there was nothing to stop her from returning the whole sum intact, if that was what he wanted. All she asked for was a chance to show what she could do.

The manservant who answered the summons was the same one who had shown her here to this room a short time ago. Face impassive, he listened to his master's instructions, then indicated to Jan that she should accompany him. She could feel the piercing gaze on her back as she followed the man from the room, and made an effort to walk tall and straight. Whatever the verdict, she would accept it with dignity. Right now that was all she had left.

The room to which she was taken lay just off the galleried landing. It left her practically speechless in its sheer luxury. Despite the heat of the early August day outside, within the thick walls of the house itself it was deliciously cool. The floor here was carpeted, the deep blue pile complemented by the paler blue silk covers and hangings on the four-poster bed. Matching window drapes were held back by twisted cords to frame a superb view of the surrounding countryside.

There was a dressing area lined with wardrobes off to one side, and off that again a beautifully equipped bathroom, complete with semi-sunken bath reached via two steps. If this was the same suite Raine would have been using, Don Felipe certainly didn't stint his employees of creature comforts, Jan granted.

Her initial eagerness to keep this job—fired to a great extent by the unanticipated opposition—was slowly giving way to doubt. Don Felipe was a man totally outside her experience of the gender. Did she really want to work for someone so obviously accustomed to ruling the roost? Taking orders was one thing, being totally under command quite another.

On the other hand, she hadn't even been offered the job yet, she reminded herself. To say the substitution had come as a surprise to him was putting it mildly. What on earth had Raine been playing at? There had been no misunderstanding. She had definitely said she'd contacted the man and arranged everything. It seemed so senseless a lie under the circumstances.

But then, who was to really know how Raine's mind worked? They had never been close, as true sisters might have been. Perhaps Jan was the fool for trusting her. It wasn't the first time Raine had dropped her in it.

Scarcely able to remember the mother who had died when she was three years old, Jan had tried her best to welcome the advent of a stepmother into her life when she was ten, but it hadn't been easy. Not that the other had been cruel to her in any way, just uninterested. It was Raine who got the hugs and kisses, the praise when she did well in school; Raine who got away with murder, simply because her mother believed she could do no wrong. Jan had often thought that things might have been different if the two of them hadn't been almost exactly the same age, although looking back now, with the perception of her twenty-three years, she doubted it.

Her father hadn't been much comfort, either. All he had seemed to think about was business. His death from a heart attack when Jan was eighteen had nevertheless left her numb with grief. The realisation that he had been about to be made bankrupt had come as another shock. The house had been all that was left untouched, which Jan's stepmother had promptly sold in order to buy a smaller, modern property and provide herself with an income. Once she found a good job, Jan had been only too happy to move out into a place of her own.

Rarely content with anything for very long, Raine had developed a wanderlust. Jan had grown accustomed to receiving boldly scrawled postcards from all over Europe; to finding her stepsister at the door every few months or so with a whole new set of adventures to relate. What she did for money, Jan had no idea. She certainly never appeared to suffer from a lack of it.

Her latest visit and her offer of this job just one short week ago had seemed like manna from heaven at the time. Jan hadn't stopped to think it out, just grasped the opportunity with both hands. The six months' advance on salary had been unusual, true, but one didn't quibble over five thousand pounds. It had been simple enough to have the plane ticket altered to her initial—and here she was.

And here she had to stay, if at all possible, came the thought, swiftly hardening into fresh resolve. Mistake or not, she had burned all her bridges in order to take this job, and she was prepared to fight to keep it.

All the same, it would be tempting providence to unpack the suitcase already deposited on the rack in the dressing-room, she decided. She would take out only what she needed for this evening, and leave the rest until she knew where she stood.

The tray of tea and small fancy cakes brought up to her at four-thirty came as a pleasant surprise. She tried to engage the young maidservant in conversation, but the girl was either too shy or had been warned against fraternisation, because she was answered only in monosyllables.

With several hours to kill before dinner, and tired anyway from the journey, she decided to refresh herself with a nap after she had eaten. Old though the bed itself might be, the mattress was a modern, interior sprung one, blissfully comfortable and supportive. Lying on top of the undercover in her slip, having carefully rolled back the heavier blue silk, Jan felt the day's tensions slowly drain from her. Just an hour or so, she promised herself sleepily. Rested, she would be far better able to cope with the situation awaiting her.

It seemed as if bare minutes had passed when she opened her eyes again. Only when she sat up, stifling a yawn, did she realise that the dimness of the room was due to the onset of evening. A glance at her watch drew a startled exclamation to her lips. Eight o'clock already! She had slept for more than three hours.

It was lucky she had awakened when she did, came the thought as she scrambled hastily to her feet. Being late for dinner would hardly have created a very good impression. Not that anything was cut and dried as yet, she recalled with a sudden dip in spirits. It was doubtful whether Don Felipe could be persuaded to change his mind, once it was made up. All she could hope was that his decision would be in her favour.

The bathroom boasted a separate shower-cubicle in addition to the bath itself. Using one of the thick Turkish towels, Jan could see herself reflected from all sides by the inset wall-mirrors. Designed by or for a regular narcissist, she thought, feeling oddly self-conscious in her repetitive nudity. The glass must have been specially treated, too, in order for it not to steam up.

By half-past eight she was dressed and ready in a lemon silk tunic, her hair hanging smooth and shining about a face only lightly touched with make-up. A single string of pearls that had belonged to her mother, together with the gold watch that had been her eighteenth birthday present from her father, was all the jewellery she wore. Jan disliked flashiness of any kind. Little and good was her motto. Taking a last look in the mirror before leaving the room, it occurred to her to wonder if black might not have been a more suitable choice for the occasion, but it was too late now to start having doubts. If Don Felipe was the man she believed him to be, he was hardly going to be swayed by minor detail, anyway.

From the gallery, the grand staircase descended in a graceful curve to the vast hall. Reaching the latter, Jan stood indecisively for a moment or two, wondering which of the many doors she should try first. She was relieved when the same young maid who had brought her the tea earlier appeared from the back regions and indicated that she should follow her.

Furnished to the degree of comfort and opulence she was coming to expect, the *salón* to which she was shown had fretted ironwork grills at the window embrasures. She was studying the Corot on the fireplace wall when Don Felipe put in an appearance. Dressed now in dark trousers and a black silk shirt opened at the throat on a glint of gold, he looked no less the master of his household.

'You're at least punctual,' he observed, his glance scanning her slender figure as she turned. 'Unusual in a woman.'

'It would hardly have been good policy to be anything else under the circumstances, *señor*,' she responded with what smoothness she could muster.

A fugitive gleam of mockery lit the dark eyes. 'True,' he acknowledged. 'You would like a drink?'

About to refuse, Jan abruptly changed her mind. She needed some kind of prop, for certain. 'Sherry would be fine,' she said, and couldn't resist tagging on, 'Spanish, of course.'

'Sweet or dry?' His tone was decidedly the latter. 'Or perhaps I may suggest the *Oloroso*?'

'Please.' She was already regretting the unsubtle retort. The Rimados sherries were world renowed. Don Felipe could be forgiven for considering her little joke rather tasteless.

She watched him as he went across to open up a cabinet and extract glasses, admiring the lithe and supple manner of his movements. Fit as a fiddle, without an ounce of excess fat on him, she judged, and was aware of a sudden curling sensation in the very pit of her stomach. It was all she could do to hang on to her equilibrium when he brought the sherry back to where she stood, handing her the crystal glass with a sardonic inclination of his head.

'To your health!' he said, raising his own glass.

Full bodied and soft, the sherry warmed her through. Don Felipe was still standing close; too close, she thought in sudden, unwonted panic. The man overwhelmed her with his sheer masculinity. She wasn't accustomed to the kind of vibes he exuded.

'You're still intent upon taking your sister's place?' he asked, not moving his gaze from her face.

Jan hesitated, not all that sure again. 'Does that mean you're offering me the job?' she countered, playing for time.

'It means,' he said, 'that I'm prepared to extend you the opportunity to prove your suitability in the same way that your sister did.'

Her brow knitted a little. 'What way is that?'

'You'll be required to undergo a full medical examination at the hands of my personal physician. I must naturally be assured of your fitness.'

'Naturally,' she echoed, trying to sound as if such a request was a normal, everyday occurrence. She was only a secretary, for heaven's sake, not a high-flying executive!

All the same, if it was a requirement of employment, then she could do little but agree. She had no doubts regarding the state of her health. What harm could it do to have the fact confirmed?

'When did you have in mind?' she asked.

'Tomorrow morning,' he said. 'Should everything prove satisfactory, the contract will be ready for your signature.' Just for the moment there was a harder glint in his eyes. 'And this time it will be fulfilled!'

Jan made an effort to pull herself together. It was hardly to be expected that he would look kindly on yet another let-down. 'Of course,' she agreed. 'My word is my bond.'

'Good—' Apparently about to add something else, he broke off as a gong sounded. 'Leave your glass here,' he advised, ignoring the fact that it was still more than half-full.

The dining-room was across the hallway. Long enough to seat at least twenty people in comfort, the intricately carved table was laid for only two. Jan found herself seated on Don Felipe's right, faced with an array of silver and crystal that would have done justice to a full banquet. Wine was poured, and there began a meal of so many different courses that she entirely lost count after the first two.

'You eat sparingly,' commented her host at one point, watching her pick at a dish of fried sole. 'Is the food not to your liking?'

'There's just too much of it,' she admitted, opting for truth in the hope that quantities at least would be adjusted. 'I'm not used to more than three courses, and only then on special occasions.' She tried a smile. 'More often that not, it's something out of a packet.'

'Perhaps that's why you're so slender,' he returned. 'A few more pounds would do you no harm.'

'It's the fashion to be slim,' she protested. 'And healthier, too!'

His shrug made light of the argument, if it could be called that. 'We'll see.' He nodded to the black-suited manservant, whom he had addressed as Juan, to take the plate away, adding in Spanish that they would progress straight to coffee.

'You said you were fluent in my language,' he said to Jan in the same tongue. 'Where did you learn?'

She made the switch smoothly. 'At night-school. There was a chance of a transfer to my former employer's Madrid office. Unfortunately, someone else finished up going.'

'A pity,' he agreed. 'You have a good command.'

'Not as good as your English.'

A smile touched his lips. 'My education was completed at Oxford. Once acquired, the accent isn't really lost. You come from Buckinghamshire, I believe?'

'Born and bred.' She looked up to thank Juan as coffee was placed before her, eliciting a somewhat surprised glance from the man. 'My family, too,' she continued, bringing her attention back to the head of the table.

He stirred cream into his coffee, and said levelly, 'I understood from your stepsister that her father was no longer living. Was she referring to her natural father or your own?'

'Both, I suppose,' Jan acknowledged. 'Mine died five years ago when Raine and I were eighteen.'

'You're the same age?' He sounded surprised. 'I should have thought you younger.'

Did that mean she acted it or looked it? wondered Jan, and wasn't sure which she would prefer.

'Why are you not married yourself, by now?' he asked unexpectedly, stampeding her into an unconsidered reply.

'Because I happen to think there are things more important than romance.'

'For a man, perhaps; not for a woman.' His gaze was too perceptive by half. 'I think you may have suffered a recent heartache.'

She made herself hold the gaze. 'Nothing that will affect my job here, *señor*.'

'That,' he said, 'is a matter of opinion.' The pause was brief, his expression difficult to read. 'You had an intimate relationship with this man?'

Twin spots of colour bloomed high on her cheekbones. With difficulty she kept her tone level. 'I doubt if that's really your business, *señor*.'

'Everything and anything to do with those I employ is my business,' he stated unequivocally. 'I take it the answer is yes?'

'No!' She was goaded beyond endurance by the cool assumption. 'No, it damn well isn't!'

She had dropped back automatically into English to emphasise the denial. She continued in that language, to add with heat, 'This job you're offering may be good, but my life prior to it is my own affair. If you can't accept that, *señor*, then we'd better part company here and now!'

His brows had risen, his whole demeanour one of autocracy. 'You will not speak to me in that manner!' he clipped.

Jan took a grip on herself, steadying her breathing by sheer effort of will. This was a different culture, came the reminder. There had to be a better way of handling the situation, even if it did mean climbing down from her stance a little.

'I apologise,' she said stiffly. 'I shouldn't have lost my temper in that way. It's just that, where I come from, people simply don't ask questions like that.'

His head inclined. 'The apology is accepted.'

'Wouldn't you be better off with one of your own countrywomen?' asked Jan on sudden impulse, and saw his mouth take a slant.

'Blood isn't the priority.' His tone altered, became businesslike. 'If you've finished your coffee, I'd suggest an early night in order to be fit for the morning. Dr Valdes will be here at eight.'

'Before breakfast?'

'Of course before breakfast. Some tests are better performed on an empty stomach. You may eat your fill,' he added, 'just as soon as he's through with you. I shall have the results by lunchtime.'

'I think you'll find them quite satisfactory,' Jan returned. 'So far as I know, I don't have a thing wrong with me.' She got up from the table, not trusting herself to say any more.

'Goodnight, *señor*.'

He had risen with her. Shades of Oxford? she wondered fleetingly.

'Goodnight,' he said.

Only when she had gained the privacy of the bedroom did she allow herself the luxury of a single, meaningful expletive. That man down there was a despot! Did she really want to work for such a person?

Yes, but what did she have to go back to? came the inevitable rejoinder. A year wasn't all that long a time, and with another five thousand pounds to add to that already held, she would be in a position to take her time looking round for another job. Odd that Don Felipe hadn't requested some proof of her actual qualifications, when she came to think of it, but no doubt he would make up for that lack in the morning before presenting the contract. In the meantime, she had better do as he said and get some more sleep.

Morning brought a renewal of doubt, swiftly dispelled by the sheer delight of the sunlit landscape seen from the window. The vineyards she had driven through yesterday stretched seemingly for miles. A white church tower and a clutch of red roofs suggested there was a fair-sized village not so very far away.

She was ready and waiting in a cotton wrap when Dr Valdes was announced on the stroke of eight. A man in his early fifties, with a pleasant but impersonal manner that soon dispelled any awkwardness, he gave her the most thorough going-over she had ever experienced in her life. It took an hour altogether, and left her feeling that no corner had been left unexplored. If she came out of this with flying colours, she could at least be assured of living a good few years, she thought humorously when it was over and the doctor had departed.

Breakfast was brought to her room almost immediately afterwards by the young maid who appeared to have been assigned to her. Her name was Yola, Jan learned, and she was the daughter of Juan, who performed the functions of butler. No more than eighteen years of age, she seemed to have little girlish zest for life about her. Too solemn by half, Jan thought, and she resolved to do something about it, given the opportunity.

There was no sign of Don Felipe when she finally went downstairs at ten o'clock. The master would be back for lunch at two, Juan informed her when asked. Until then she was free to do as she wished.

Taking him at his word, she spent the next hour or so wandering from room to magnificent room, losing her bearings from time to time. All this for one man was ridiculous, she reflected, growing ever more bemused. There was even a ballroom, beautifully kept, yet obviously rarely used.

Eventually, she found her way outside, emerging from dim coolness into brilliant sunlight and burning heat. The grounds were extensive, the lawns sparkling with moisture from the automatic sprinkling system. Passing through a stone archway, she found herself standing on the edge of a swimming-pool designed to look like a natural formation, with plants and trees surrounding it. She had brought along a swim-suit in the hope that she might find time and opportunity to visit the coast, but this was going to be even better!

Stop counting your chickens, she cautioned herself at that point. You can't be sure you even have the job yet!

The blue-tinted water was a temptation. Don Felipe surely wouldn't object if she took a swim? Going back inside, she went swiftly to her room and changed into the black and white striped suit, covering herself with a short towelling robe and sliding her feet into raffia mules.

Apart from a man tending the flower troughs around a pergola, and another cutting back some high shrubbery in the middle distance, there was no one around to see her slip across the wide rear patio and through the archway. Casting aside the robe, she slid into the pool at what turned out to be the shallow end, and struck out in an effortless crawl. The water felt delicious—warm enough for there to be no shock on immersion, yet rejuvenating in effect.

She wanted to stay here, she thought, turning on to her back to float after a while. Who wouldn't want to live and work in such surroundings? Don Felipe might be a bit of an autocrat, but she could surely adjust to that for a year? All it would take was a little diplomacy. Not exactly her strong point, true, only well worth practising, considering what she stood to gain.

With eyes half closed against the sun's glare, it took her a little time to realise that the tall, dark shadow on the edge of the pool was not another tree. Don Felipe stood with hands thrust into the pockets of his white trousers, drawing the material taut across his thighs. The deep blue shirt was open half-way down his chest to reveal a thick growth of hair. A small gold medallion nestled in the centre.

'You enjoy the water?' he asked.

Jan came upright, using hands and feet to keep herself afloat as she looked up the length of the lean, fit body. 'Very much,' she said, and then quickly, 'I realise I should perhaps have asked permission, but—'

'The pool is here to be used,' he interrupted, sounding surprised. 'There's no permission necessary. It is, however, time we concluded our affairs.'

'Of course.' She made for the side, her heart thudding when he moved to extend a hand to her. 'You'll get wet,' she protested.

'So I get wet.' The shrug was dismissive. 'Come.'

She felt the tensile strength in his fingers as they closed about hers, the power in his arms as he hauled her easily from the water. For a brief moment she was held there in front of him, her eyes on a level with his jawline, her whole body trembling with an emotion she didn't want to examine too closely.

'Thank you,' she managed, and moved away, reaching for the robe she had flung over a stone seat. Only when it was on and the belt securely tied did she feel able to look him in the eye. 'When you say conclude, do you mean I'm to be sent away?'

'No.' The hard-boned features were impassive. 'I called on Dr Valdes on my way home. He found your health excellent.'

Her heart jerked again, not entirely with relief. 'You're saying I have the job?'

'It would appear so. If you'd like to dress, there will be time to complete the formalities before lunch.'

'Yes, of course.' She fell into step beside him as he moved towards the archway, trying to exude confidence. Once that contract was signed she would be committed. A year suddenly seemed an awful big lump out of her life.

She had to stop this vacillating, she told herself severely. A chance like this might never come her way again. She couldn't afford to turn it down for want of a little backbone.

Don Felipe left her in the hall. She was to come to the study, he said, as soon as she was ready. Once in her room, Jan took a quick shower and dressed in a neat cotton skirt and matching shirt in a blue print that went with her eyes. Her resolve was firm now. She was going to take this job—whatever. Don Felipe might prove to be a strict employer, but he would be a fair one. Of that she was reasonably certain.

He was standing at the window when she entered the study at his invitation. Turning, he scanned her features, his expression difficult to decipher.

'The contract is there on the desk,' he said. 'You wish to check the terms before you sign it?'

Jan shook her head. Having come this far, she wasn't going to start backing out now, no matter what. 'I know all I need to know.' Taking up the pen laid ready, she wrote her name in the appropriate place, putting it down again with a faint exhalation of breath. 'There you are. Signed and sealed!'

He moved to take up the paper and glance at the signature. 'What does the J stand for?' he asked.

'Janine,' she answered. 'But everyone calls me Jan for short.'

He made no comment to that, sliding the contract into a desk-drawer, which he then locked.

'Now we go and eat,' he said.

Lunch was a much lighter meal than dinner, Jan was thankful to find. She was hungry after her swim, and did full justice to the prawn dish served as an appetiser. Wine was freely available, today a dry white that was delightfully light on the palate. She found herself relaxing under its influence.

'I suppose we should get round to discussing my exact duties,' she murmured when she was half-way down the second glass. 'Naturally, I'm prepared to begin right away.'

Don Felipe gave her an odd glance. 'So I should hope. Tonight will be soon enough.'

It was Jan's turn to glance, her brows drawing together. 'Tonight?'

'Of course.' His own brows lifted a fraction. 'Unless you'd prefer this afternoon?'

Some element of doubt began slowly unfurling deep down in the very pit of her stomach. She gazed at him, her eyes suddenly darker, lips slightly parted as if to take in more air. 'I'm—not sure I understand,' she got out.

He studied her in silence for a long moment, his expression undergoing a subtle alteration. When he did speak, it was in tones she found distinctly unnerving. 'Exactly what,' he asked, 'did you think this contract of ours entailed?'

'Why—secretarial duties,' she said. 'Raine told me it was a personal secretary you needed.'

'Did she, indeed?' There was anger in the comment, along with something else Jan couldn't quite define. 'It seems your stepsister has little regard for the truth.'

'Why?' The question was torn from her, her mind unable to grasp what possible alternatives there could be to the job she had believed was hers. 'If it isn't a secretary, what exactly is it that you do want?'

Dropped levelly and precisely into the pause, each word was a hammer blow to her heart.

'I want a son,' he said.

CHAPTER TWO

How long Jan just sat there staring at him, she couldn't afterwards have said for certain. Her mind was whirling, her senses numbed.

'Is this some kind of joke?' she stammered at length.

From his tone, the idea didn't even merit novelty value. 'I don't joke about such matters. Your sister was fully aware of the requirements.'

'I don't believe that,' she stated flatly, attempting to pull herself together. 'She *couldn't* have known!'

'She's already proved herself a liar in one respect,' he reminded her. 'Why not another?'

'Because no one in their right mind would contemplate what you're suggesting,' she burst out, abandoning all effort towards constraint. 'Me, least of all!'

'You already signed the contract,' he returned hardily. 'You asked to take your sister's place, and that is what you will do.'

'No way!' She was on her feet, pulses racing, heart thudding painfully against her ribs. 'I'm leaving this place right now!'

'You are not.' He had risen with her, his eyes like black stones in the taut olive skin. 'We have an agreement; you will fulfil it.'

'You can't make me!' Trembling, the hand clutching the back of her chair white-knuckled, she added with emphasis, 'There's no court in the world that would uphold that paper I signed!'

'No court in England, perhaps,' he countered. 'But this is Spain. My country.'

'Even so——'

The impatient gesture cut her off in mid sentence. 'No matter. *I* say you'll fulfil your obligations. I warned you I would brook no further retraction.'

'I didn't know,' she came back desperately. 'You have to believe me!'

'I do.' He said it quite calmly, the anger well under control. 'That quarrel is with your sister, no one else. You were given every opportunity to read the contract before you signed. You chose not to do so.'

'That makes me a fool,' she returned with bitterness, 'not an idiot! If it's a son you're after, why not try it the normal way, with a wife?'

'I have no wish to marry,' he stated. 'All I want is the child. Without a son of my own, the title and estates would pass to my cousins, who don't bear the name of Rimados.'

Jan shook her head fiercely. 'I'm not interested in your reasons. I'm not interested in anything you have to offer! I'm going home, and you can't stop me!'

'You think not?' His tone was silky, but no less dangerous for it. 'And how would you propose to leave here?'

'The way I came.'

'By car? Driven by whom, may I ask? My staff are loyal. They would do nothing against my wishes.'

'Then I'll walk to the village and get transport from there.'

'All of the villagers are in my employ,' he said. 'You'll find no help there. Jerez is more than twenty kilometres away. Do you believe you could walk that far?'

Blue eyes refused to drop before the hard mockery. 'I'll do anything that's necessary to get me away from here!'

'Enough!' If there had been any tolerance at all in his manner, he was totally devoid of it now. 'You'll sit down and finish your meal, and then we'll discuss the matter more fully.'

She gazed at him wordlessly, recognising the finality, yet still not prepared to accept it. The whole thing was unbelievable. To bear this man's child as part of a paid contract—it didn't even bear thinking about!

'It would be illegitimate, anyway,' she said with deliberation. 'A bastard—isn't that the correct term?'

His eyes acquired a glint of steel. 'I should naturally make arrangements to adopt the child legally. After the birth, you'll receive the remaining ten thousand pounds and free passage back to England.'

Jan's mind whirled again, the final words scarcely penetrating. '*Ten* thousand?'

'That was the figure agreed. Twenty thousand pounds sterling, one half in advance.'

So Raine had not only lied to her about the whole deal, but kept back five thousand pounds for herself, Jan acknowledged, feeling suddenly sickened. The money wasn't important, but how could Raine justify this situation she had landed her with?

The truth was that, so far as Raine was concerned, the end justified the means, came the bitter reflection. It always had—although she had never gone this far before.

Don Felipe was watching her with narrowed gaze, his perception too acute to miss the subtle change in her manner. 'She deceived you in this, too, I gather,' he said. 'That comes as no great surprise.'

'You're quite wrong.' The denial was instinctive. 'I was simply thinking that another ten thousand sounded pretty paltry for what you're asking.'

Both denial and insult were ignored. 'Your loyalty does you credit,' he said. 'However, this too is a matter between you and your sister.' The pause was brief, his tone a threat in itself. 'Do you sit down as I asked, or do I make you?'

He could, there was little doubt about that. Jan chose dignity in preference to loss of it, regaining her seat with a sense of helplessness. There had to be some way of getting through to him. None of this was her fault. Who could possibly have guessed that this 'job' was not all it seemed?

'What would have happened if Raine hadn't sent me in her place?' she asked after a moment or two. 'I mean, you could scarcely have enforced the contract under British law.'

'The law would have had no bearing,' he returned levelly. 'She would have been brought back.'

'You mean kidnapped?'

'If that had been the only way.'

'Even if she'd returned the money?' Jan persisted.

'The money is not the issue,' he said. 'Unlike you, she accepted the proposal in full knowledge of what would be required of her. Had she not had the foresight to provide an acceptable substitute, she would in a very short time be experiencing my displeasure.'

'Such an escape!' The sarcasm itself was a defence. 'And you really think her disappearance would have caused no comment?'

'From what I know of your sister's life-style, the answer to that question is yes.' He paused, his mouth taking on a certain irony. 'Physically, she met all the

criteria, but she was perhaps a little lacking in other ways.
When I take you, I'll know there has been no other man
before me. That fact alone is worth perhaps a further
five thousand pounds.'

Jan felt her whole face flame. 'Damn you!' she said
viciously. 'You have no right——'

'I have every right.' He wasn't giving an inch. 'You
gave me the right. The sooner you accustom yourself to
that fact, the better for all concerned. Now eat.'

If she'd been starving, Jan couldn't have forced a
single morsel of food between her lips at that moment.
She felt totally out of her depth. What kind of a man
was it who could contemplate such an arrangement?
More to the point, how did she get out of the situation?

As if on cue, the door opened to admit Juan bearing
a tray loaded with fresh dishes. Don Felipe indicated
that the present unfinished dishes should be removed,
reaching out himself to refill Jan's glass with the crystal
clear wine as fluffy Spanish omelettes were placed before
them. Jan briefly contemplated an appeal to the man
serving her, but one glance at the expressionless olive
features soon dispelled any hope of help from that
quarter. Whether he was aware of his master's plans for
her remained an open question, but there was little, if
any, chance of turning him against the man on whom
both he and his daughter relied for an income. The same
would in all probability apply to the whole of the staff—
even the villagers themselves. She was on her own.

'Supposing the child turned out to be a girl?' she
suggested when the servant had left the room again.
'That would hardly help your cause.'

'Only males have been born to the Rimados line in
more than two hundred years,' came the unmoved response. 'I doubt there's much danger of my changing

the pattern now. However, in the unlikely event, the contract would simply be extended to cover a second child, with the same conditions governing.'

'Then all I'd have to do is keep on having girls and I'd be set for life.'

'Fortunately, the deciding factor has nothing to do with the female,' he returned drily. 'Perhaps a few lessons in basic biology wouldn't go amiss.'

'This whole thing is ridiculous!' she flung at him, unable to contain herself any longer. 'Did you never hear the old proverb about leading a horse to water?'

His smile held sudden amusement. 'You're saying I'll have to use force?'

She kept back the flush by sheer effort of will. 'Yes, I am.'

'I don't expect it to be necessary,' he said, 'but should it come to that...' His shrug left no doubt as to his meaning.

'You're depraved!' she accused with vehemence. 'Do you know that?'

The steel was back in his eyes again. 'You may believe it, if it comforts you. I prefer to look on it as expedience. You can provide what I need.'

'Supposing I'm barren. Have you thought of *that*?'

'Unlikely. Dr Valdes could find no reason why you shouldn't bear a dozen healthy children. I ask only the one son.'

'Forbearing of you.' Jan was silent for a moment, gathering her resources. 'Everything else aside,' she said at length, 'do you really think I'd consent to simply walking away afterwards? The child would be mine, too, remember.'

'That also was written into the contract. You give up all rights in exchange for the financial settlement.'

Arguing that point was a waste of time, she conceded. It was a hypothetical question, anyway, because she had no intention of allowing matters to get that far.

'The money will be returned,' she said. 'That, so far as I'm concerned, breaks any contract.'

'The whole of it?' He smiled sardonically as she bit her lip. 'What exactly *was* the amount passed on to you?'

'It doesn't matter.' She tried another tack, searching for some chink in the armour. 'Why Raine in the first place? Surely, if you're going to do this at all, it would be better to keep the blood pure?'

'I have English blood myself,' he declared. 'From my mother's side. I've no objection to a little more dilution. Environment shapes the character. My son will be Spanish in thought, word and deed, whatever his colouring. Apart from which,' he tagged on, 'finding a participant both suitable *and* willing among my own countrywomen would have been difficult.'

'But I'm *not* willing! Doesn't that make any difference to you?'

'Your stepsister was—or certainly appeared to be.' He was growing impatient, his mouth taking on a line that advised caution. 'We're going around in circles. Must I keep on repeating myself?'

'Must *I*?' The wine had given her courage—or at least removed inhibition. Eyes sparking, she brought her fist down sharply on the table, making the glassware dance. 'I'd kill myself before I let you touch me!'

'Life is sweet,' he returned, unmoved by the display. 'I think you may change your mind. Tonight, and every night until I can be assured you're with child, I shall come to you. If you wish me to be gentle with you, then you must act accordingly. Otherwise...' He left it there, draining his glass with an air of finality.

Jan sat motionless. Her throat was so dry, she could barely swallow. He meant every word, there was no doubt about that in her mind any more. How could Raine have done this to her? How could she have agreed to it in the first place, if it came to that? Not that any amount of wondering was going to help her own present situation.

'I'd like to be alone,' she forced out through stiff lips. 'Do you have any objection if I go to my room?'

'You may go wherever you like, providing you don't attempt to leave the estate,' he returned. 'If you require anything, you have only to call one of the servants. They have instructions to give you every assistance.'

Except for passage out of here, she thought hollowly. She rose and left the room, passing Juan, who was bringing in dessert, with her head held high. She had the rest of the day to come up with some plan. There had to be a way of escape somehow!

Despite its size, the bedroom felt claustrophobic. With the heavy oak door closed and locked she would be totally trapped. That Don Felipe was capable of having her locked in should the need arise, she didn't for a moment doubt. He was capable of anything.

Any further appeal to his sympathies was obviously going to be a complete waste of time. So far as he was concerned, she was bought and paid for—his to do with as he wished. Any attraction she might have felt towards the man had long since flown. He was cold, ruthless and totally without honour. The thought of what was to come if she didn't get out of here contracted every nerve in her body.

Think! she told herself fiercely.

Yola's arrival with refreshment at four-thirty found her lying listlessly across the bed. The Spanish girl said little, but there was a certain quality in her glance that made Jan wonder if she was aware of her predicament. Briefly, she contemplated attempting to enlist the girl's aid, but the chances of success were too limited to take the risk. Her only possible recourse at the moment was to play for more time, and how she was to do that she still wasn't sure.

By nightfall she was ready to try anything. Dressed in off-white linen, she made her way downstairs to the *salón*. Her captor was already in residence, a drink to hand. He rose when she entered the room, his light-weight suit an echo of her own choice in both colour and material. There was even a glint of something approaching humour in the glance he ran over her.

'A rare communion,' he observed. 'You would like a drink?'

'Gin,' she returned with deliberation. 'On the rocks, please.'

He poured the drink without comment, taking ice from a silver bucket set ready on a tray. Bringing the glass across to where she had seated herself on a deep sofa, he paused to pick up his own drink, taking a seat at her side.

'I think it is time we came to an understanding of each other,' he said.

Jan forced herself to sit quite still and not jerk away from contact with the muscular thigh so close to her own. She could feel the warmth of him, catch the elusive scent of aftershave. The hand holding his glass was long-fingered and lean, the wrist strong beneath the crisp shirt cuff. Wafer thin, the gold watch he was wearing was almost certainly a Rolex. Money meant nothing to this man. He had lived all his life with an abundance of it.

'The only kind of understanding I ask for,' she said huskily, 'is that you let me go.'

He shook his head. 'That would leave me back where I began. The arrangement must stand, but perhaps I was a little harsh in my judgement earlier. I'm willing to give you time to come to terms with what is expected of you.'

Jan looked at him swiftly. 'How much time?'

'A few days.'

'How generous!'

His sigh suggested a fast-waning tolerance. 'I'm trying to be. If you'd prefer, we can revert to the original plan.'

She took a grip on herself. Any reprieve was better than none. A few days would at least give her a chance to come up with something.

'I'm in no hurry,' she got out.

'Not for anything,' came the dry agreement. 'Tell me, is it just my attentions you fear, or those of any man?'

Blue eyes dropped to view the contents of the glass in her hand, her expression carefully controlled. 'I happen to consider love an essential ingredient in lovemaking.'

'Not so. Attraction, yes. Had I not found you appealing to the eye, I couldn't have accepted the exchange.'

'Obviously you found Raine appealing to the eye, too,' she said, stifling the retort that trembled on her lips. 'How did you and she meet?'

'She crashed her car into mine almost outside the gates,' he returned. 'What else could I do but bring her here to recover? It took a week for repairs to her vehicle to be effected.'

'During which time you persuaded her to accept your proposition?'

His shrug was brief. 'She took little persuading. When she left it was on the understanding that she straightened out her affairs in England. There was no mention of a man awaiting her return.'

'Alan's proposal came right out of the blue,' Jan responded. 'You can hardly blame her for preferring marriage to what you were offering.' She cast a glance at the hard profile. 'Would you really have gone after her?'

'The same way I'll come after you, should you attempt to run away,' he promised hardily. 'And with the same consequences she would have suffered had she been brought back.'

If she managed to get away, she thought fiercely, wild horses wouldn't drag her back! The first place she would make for was a police station. That contract wasn't worth the paper it was written on!

The hand that took hold of her chin to lift her face was unyielding in intent. Jan felt her knees go weak at the look in his eyes.

'Whatever you may be plotting in that mind of yours,' he warned, 'don't attempt it. I make no idle threats.'

'So what would you do?' she challenged, fighting the effect he was having on her. 'Have me beaten?'

'You would be beaten, yes,' he agreed, 'but by myself, not others.'

'And no doubt you'd take great pleasure in it!'

'Not in the way you mean. You have a lot of spirit,' he added on a slightly softer note. 'I'd hate to break it. Obey me, and there'll be no need.'

Jan forced back the heated words rising to her lips. She was going to get nowhere by defying him. Women obviously were, or should be, the subservient sex in his estimation. A little subterfuge was called for, galling though it would be to pretend anything other than the detestation she felt for the whole affair.

'It seems,' she said, 'that you have me backed into a corner, *señor.*'

'Felipe,' he corrected. 'You will call me Felipe from now on.' It was impossible to tell whether he accepted her apparent submission. Still holding her by the chin, he dropped his head to brush his lips across hers in a gesture that sent a sensation like molten fire through her veins. Involuntarily she tensed, her nails curling into the palms of her hands. Such a fleeting caress, yet it left a totally new awareness in its wake. She gazed at him numbly when he released her.

'Unawakened, perhaps, but not without normal responses,' he observed dispassionately. 'I don't think it will be necessary to use force on you, *mi querida*, when the times comes.'

Faced with the emotions he could rouse in her with a single kiss, Jan was beginning to doubt it, too. Contrary to the beliefs she had always held dear, mind and body were not all that closely allied. All the more reason for her to get away, she thought desperately. To be taken by this man would be bad enough; to actually find herself responding to his approaches was not even to be contemplated!

She made every effort over dinner to lull him into believing she had given up any idea of escape. As a conversationalist, he was excellent company. Several times she found herself on the verge of forgetting why she was here, and had to forcibly catch herself up.

He, too, appeared relaxed. Shorn of the grimness with which he had first greeted her, his face looked younger, she thought, the bone structure itself less forbidding. In other circumstances, she could well imagine she might even have found him quite devastating. He was certainly like no other man she had ever met before.

'I always thought Latin families tended to live together,' she murmured curiously over coffee. 'This seems such a huge place for just one.'

'My mother died in childbirth,' he returned. 'My father never married again. He was killed in an air disaster some years ago. The aunts and uncles and cousins who survive have homes of their own.'

'But none of them close enough to be named your successor?'

'None who bear the name. I've already told you that. My father's two brothers died in an influenza epidemic when they were quite young, and left no issue.'

'Your family has borne a lot of tragedy,' she said with a flash of genuine sympathy.

His shrug was dismissive. 'We must all die eventually.'

'But better later rather than sooner,' remarked Jan, then added pointedly, 'Is the reason you've never married yourself because you don't really like women?'

A corner of the strong mouth flicked upwards. 'You suspect me of other tendencies?'

That, Jan thought, was about the only thing she *could* be sure of, where this man was concerned. 'No,' she said. 'Not for a moment.'

'I'm relieved.' He paused, his gaze resting on her face. 'My reasons for not marrying are personal, but they don't include a dislike of women in general. On the contrary, I believe female companionship to be of the utmost importance.'

She returned his gaze without a flicker. 'I take it you mean in your bed?'

This time the amusement was edged. 'You take a lot of liberties.'

'No more,' she retaliated, 'than you do.'

'Except that I'm entitled.'

'Only from your own viewpoint. Money might purchase the body, *señor*, but it can't buy the soul!'

'Such a poetic turn of phrase in a race usually so prosaic.' His regard had sharpened into speculation. 'I think there may be more to you than at first meets the eye. Perhaps our relationship may prove fruitful in more ways than the one!'

Their relationship wasn't going to last long enough to bear any kind of fruit, Jan promised herself, trying not to acknowledge the involuntary reaction. He could make his voice so soft, so sensuous when he chose. When he made love to a woman, came the sneaking thought, it would be with finesse as well as passion. Her body felt hot and restless, her skin tingling. It was not the first time she had experienced physical attraction, but never before had she felt quite like this. She was even aware of a fleeting temptation to let matters take their course.

Disgust followed swiftly in the wake of the latter emotion. How could she so much as think in that way? Felipe de Rimados had no feeling for her as an individual. She was simply a means to an end. He and Raine would have made a perfect pair—both of them totally ruthless in their self-interest.

'The night is fine,' he said unexpectedly into the silence. 'Perhaps we should take a brandy out to the patio?'

'I don't think so, thanks.' All Jan wanted at this moment was to be on her own again, away from his disturbing presence. 'I'm not a brandy fan,' she tagged on weakly.

'Some other alternative, then.' He wasn't about to let her go so easily, that was apparent from his tone. 'You'd prefer that I gave you no choice in the matter?' he asked on the silky note she was coming to recognise and treat with caution. 'A little fresh air will be good for both of us.'

Sighing, she gave in. 'If you say so. Only I don't want anything else to drink.'

That refusal was accepted without argument. Summoning Juan by pressure on the bell set into the table-top, he ordered that brandy be taken outside, then got to his feet.

'Come,' he said.

The patio could be reached via all the rear-facing rooms. Semi-covered at one end by jutting beams heavily laced in bougainvillaea, it had deep, comfortable chairs set around a low central table. Juan brought out the crystal decanter and two glasses on a tray, and departed again, leaving only the cicadas to break the stillness of the night air. A dozen or more different scents assailed Jan's nostrils from the flower-beds close by. Lacking the fierce heat and humidity of the daylight hours, the temperature was delicious.

'It's so lovely out here!' she exclaimed impulsively, forgetting her initial reluctance in the sheer pleasure of the experience. 'We get so few opportunities to sit outdoors in the evenings back home.'

'Even here there are drawbacks,' Felipe responded easily. 'But the mosquitoes appear to be absent tonight. Are you sure you won't change your mind about the brandy? It's a rather special brand.'

Why not? she thought. It would at least give her something to do with her hands.

'All right,' she said. 'Just a very small one, though.'

He poured for them both, placing the smaller measure before her and leaning back in his chair to roll his own glass between his hands for a moment or two before sampling the contents. Taking a cautious sip herself, Jan felt an immediate glow as the liquid slid smoothly down over her tongue, a slight release of tension. No situation was so bad that it couldn't be got over, or around. All she needed was a little time, and that he had given her.

Thinking of him as Felipe was difficult. Stealing a glance at the hard profile, she wondered briefly what it might be like to have him as a friend instead of an enemy. Except that enemy was hardly the right word, either. By his own lights, he was acting in a perfectly honourable fashion. Trying to persuade him to see things her way was no good at all, when he couldn't even conceive of any wrongdoing, yet to accept his dictum would be against every principle she had. A baby wasn't a chattel to be bought and sold over the bargaining counter; it was a human being with needs and rights of its own. Never in a million years could she change her mind on that score.

'I've already told you that you've nothing to fear from me tonight,' he said on a sardonic note, startling her out of her reverie. 'So you may stop looking sideways at me with such trepidation.'

'As a matter of fact,' she said without haste, 'I was trying to decide whether you really would take a woman against her will.'

'Is that so?' He sounded faintly amused. 'And your conclusions?'

'I didn't actually get as far as drawing any.'

'Then I'll save you from further speculation on the subject. The choice will be entirely your own.'

'Meaning, if I'm hurt it will be my own fault?'

'Of course.' No lights had been switched on, in order, Jan supposed, not to attract the insect life. His eyes were in shadow, his expression impossible to read. 'The first time doesn't have to be the painful experience so often imagined. Any man should be capable of deflowering a virgin with gentleness and care. It's only the insensitive who consider speed an asset.'

A pulse was beating at her temple, the blood singing in her ears. Talking like this with a man was a new experience. It excited her, stirred her, made her whole body feel as if she had ants running everywhere just under the skin. She wanted him to go on, just to listen to that voice of his, so soft that it was almost a caress in itself. Pulling herself up and out of the danger zone was an effort.

'Sensitivity wouldn't appear to be all that high on your priority list,' she said thickly.

Putting down the glass, she got up and went to stand gazing out into the moonlit night, while she tried to steady her leaping pulses. It wasn't right that he could affect her in this way when her every instinct deplored his intention. She needed to run, and keep on running. Anywhere, providing it was away from here!

She hadn't heard him move, but he was suddenly there behind her, his hands warm on her shoulders through the thin material of her dress as he drew her against him. His lips sought the pulse still throbbing at her temple, trailing a delicate passage down over her cheek to the point of her jaw, then pushing aside the heavy fall of her hair to explore the fluttering skin behind her earlobe. Jan couldn't struggle; she couldn't do anything but stand there and try to retain some measure of detachment from the sensations threatening to swamp her. If she moved at all, it would only be to bring herself even closer to the warm, hard body at her back.

'You see,' he murmured. 'It won't be so difficult. Perhaps, after all——'

'No, please!' She was terrified that he was going to suggest they rescind on the few days' grace. 'You promised me time!'

'So I did.' His tone altered, became mocking again, his hands dropping away from her. 'One week, then we seal our bargain, ready or not.'

A week from now she wouldn't be here, she told herself, swallowing on the dryness in her throat. She dared not be here. Her strength of mind was already proving unequal to the demands likely to be made on it.

CHAPTER THREE

In the following days, Jan learned to find her way around the house and more immediate grounds. With perseverance, she gradually began drawing Yola out of her shell, although the girl would spend no more than a few moments indulging in idle chat before finding some task to perform. Whether she was aware of the true situation was difficult to tell. Jan couldn't bring herself to ask her outright, mostly because she could think of no way of phrasing the question. With regard to the rest of the staff, there was no doubt at all. Wherever she went, there was always one or other of them in sight.

Felipe had made no attempt to come near her in any intimate fashion since that evening on the terrace, but she sometimes caught him watching her with a brooding look in his eyes. Most mornings he was out, returning for the long and leisurely luncheon that merged into the afternoon siesta, then disappearing again until dinner. Where he went, or what he did during those hours, Jan had no idea. She hardly saw him sitting behind an office desk, yet who was to know? Nothing about her captor was predictable.

By the middle of the week he had given her she was becoming increasingly desperate. It would just have to be a night-time escape, she reckoned. There were horses in the stable block a few hundred yards away from the main house. It would be easier to saddle one of those and ride out than to attempt stealing keys to one of the cars. Her riding experience was limited, but enough surely to get her as far as Jerez, where she could obtain transport through to Seville and a flight home?

Luckily she had enough traveller's cheques to see her back to England. The majority of her luggage, of course, she would have to abandon. A small enough price to pay for her freedom. Once home again she would ensure her safety from pursuit by going to the police. Their reaction she could at least be sure of. And after that, to Madam Raine for a refund of the money she had taken, and the return of the whole amount to settle accounts for good. Only then would she dare to breathe easily again.

The disappearance of her passport from her room was something she had not anticipated. Yola denied all knowledge of its whereabouts when asked, but she avoided Jan's eyes.

Felipe had gone to the study after lunch. He looked up, startled, from the desk where he was writing when she burst in, his brows drawing together.

'I heard no knock,' he said.

'Probably because I didn't knock.' She was too incensed to care about such niceties. 'You took my passport!' she accused.

'True,' he agreed imperturbably. 'An insurance, you might say, against your departure.'

'I wasn't planning on leaving,' she denied. 'How can I, when you have me watched the whole time?'

'In which case you hardly need your passport,' came the smooth reply, ignoring the latter question. 'It will be quite safe, I assure you.' He paused. 'Was there anything else you had to say?'

'Nothing,' she retorted bitterly, 'that you'd want to hear.'

'In which case, I have matters to take care of.' Looking at her, he seemed to relent a little. 'Later, when things are settled between us, we might go into Jerez some evening to watch the flamenco. You'd like that?'

'A reward for good behaviour?' she queried, hating him the more for his assumption. 'Don't count on anything!'

'You have three more days,' he returned, voice gaining a rougher edge. 'Or should I say nights? You'd do better not to anger me too much, unless you wish to forfeit them.'

'Damn you!' she said forcibly, and closed the door on him, leaning against it for a moment to regain some semblance of control over her emotions. He wasn't going to stop her leaving. Not this way! There was sure to be a British Consul in Seville. They would have to help her.

If there was one consolation to be obtained from the confiscation of her passport, it was that Felipe would no longer be anticipating any move on her part. Well, she would show him. She would show them all! And it had to be tonight.

There was little preparation she could make. What few items she could take with her were packed into her largest shoulder-bag, which she hid behind the dressing-chest.

The riding school where she had taken a few lessons had insisted on the pupils doing everything for themselves, including saddling and bridling their own mount. That experience would stand her in good stead. Her only worry was if a guard was placed on the stables at night. The horses were a specially bred mixture of Arab, Spanish and English stock, Felipe had told her, and extremely valuable. He had offered her the use of one of them, but she had denied any ability in that line. Hopefully, she would be well on her way to Seville before it was discovered that one of the animals was missing.

There had been odd moments during the past few evenings when she had come dangerously close to forgetting her position. Felipe could charm the birds down out of the trees when he chose to exercise that facet of his personality. Tonight she allowed herself no such relaxation. Dinner was eaten in near silence, his conversational overtures answered in monosyllables.

'You may be able to keep me here, but you can't make me like it,' she retorted when he finally lost patience with her. 'I'm not one of your minions put on earth to serve the lord and master! I'm a British subject, and I'll act like one!'

'You're a shrew,' he declared baldly. 'I shall enjoy making you draw those sharp little teeth of yours.'

'I shan't fight you, if that's what you're hoping for.' Her tone was cutting. 'When it comes to brute strength, I'm obviously not equipped to compete. Contrary to your undoubted opinion, that's the only way in which the male is superior!'

Mockery infiltrated the anger in his eyes for a moment. 'I wouldn't dispute your intelligence, simply your use of it. Is it logical to challenge my authority when I so obviously have the upper hand in this instance?'

'Is it logical,' she flashed, 'to expect a foreigner to accept your dictate just for the telling? Is it logical to believe you can keep me incarcerated here without repercussion of any kind? Supposing I fulfil your terms? What's to stop me bringing in the authorities after you throw me out, and reclaiming the child?'

The muscles about his mouth tautened ominously again. 'Nothing at all, except that I would still have your agreement on paper. No court here would grant custody to a mother willing to rent out her womb for financial gain, regardless of whether or not she changed her mind after the event.'

'*Willing* being the operative word. It was a total misunderstanding, and you know it!'

'Your word against mine.' He spoke with cruel calculation. 'You'd find none of my people willing to testify against me.'

He was telling her nothing she didn't already suspect, but hearing it put into words made it all the more certain. Not that it was going to come to that, of course. There would be no child, no contract. After tonight, she would never see him again. Something knotted deep inside her at the thought.

'You're despicable,' she said, with a contempt directed as much her own way for feeling even the slightest pang over leaving him.

'I'm many things,' he returned. 'At this moment, I'm close to dealing with you the way my forebears would have dealt with any woman who dared to speak in such a manner.'

He was more than capable of carrying out the threat, Jan conceded. Retreat went against the grain, but better that than the alternative.

'I'm sorry,' she forced out. 'I got carried away. I can't be like your women, and you shouldn't expect it.'

The apology produced no noticeable mollification. 'I've given you more leeway than you'll ever appreciate. But no more. Tonight you begin your duties.'

'No!' She was desperate now to undo the damage. 'You promised me a week!'

His glance held impatience. 'What difference is three more days going to make?'

She said it without conscious forethought. 'Perhaps a great deal. If I'm fighting anything, it's my own feelings. I need a little more time to come to terms with them, that's all.'

He considered her thoughtfully, his expression undergoing an indefinable change. 'You're trying to tell me my attentions may not after all be as repugnant to you as you suggest?'

'Is that so difficult to believe?' she countered. 'You knew the other night when you kissed me how it affected me. I—I've never known a man like you before.'

'You've never known a man, full stop,' he responded. 'Just boys who taught you nothing.' He paused. 'So, show me how you feel,' he invited. 'Come here to me now, and return the kiss.'

If she refused, Jan thought wryly, she would be giving herself away. Heart thudding, breathing suddenly harder to come by, she got to her feet and crossed the narrow area of floor between their respective chairs, bending down to press her lips fleetingly to the olive cheek. For a moment he made no move, then two hands like steel vices reached up to grasp her by the arms, pulling her down across his knees to hold her with her head resting in the crook of his arm.

'*This*,' he said, 'is a kiss, *querida*.'

His mouth was a flame, brushing aside her will-power and turning her whole world upside-down. Her lips parted, answered, gave him free rein of the inner sweetness. She who had always shied away from any use of the tongue when being kissed now found herself welcoming that very intrusion, seeking union with the tempting, tormenting probe, sliding her arms about his neck to bring him closer, everything else forgotten but the warmth rising through her veins.

The feel of his hand at her breast was no shock because she wanted it there—wanted it everywhere. His
fingers were sensitive, making her moan against his lips
in swift arousal. She yearned for his touch on her bare
skin, imagining the sensation as he brushed her aching
nipple, the encircling caress.

She was bereft when he removed both hand and lips
to look down at her with enigmatic eyes. He was
breathing a little harder himself, but was still in complete control.

'Either you learn very fast,' he said, 'or I was wrong
in my assessment. How often have you allowed a man
to caress you in this way?'

'Never,' she said truthfully.

He shook his head. 'I find that difficult to accept.
You were willing, even eager for more—much more. If
I had chosen, I could have taken you without protest.
You'd deny that?'

It was beyond her right now to deny anything. 'No,'
she said on a husky note. 'It's as I told you. You make
me feel the way no man has ever managed to.' She attempted a shaky little smile. 'There have even been times
when I believed I might be frigid.'

'Even with the man you loved?' he asked softly.

'I was never in love with him.' And that was true, too,
she realised. Gary had made the running in their relationship; all she had done was go along with him. His
kisses had certainly never aroused one tenth of the
emotions still churning around inside her now. 'It was
a mistake,' she tagged on.

Felipe had made no attempt to set her back on her
feet, his arm firm behind her head. From where she lay,
Jan could study every detail of the strongly moulded
mouth, recalling the feel of it on hers with an uncon-

trollable tremor. If he'd continued, it would probably be all over now. And how would she have felt about that? At least she still retained some measure of self-respect.

'If it's as you say,' he murmured, 'why should you wish to wait any longer for what must eventually happen?'

That was a question for which she had no logical answer. It was even more essential that she get away tonight, she thought, and hoped her eyes revealed no hint of her plans.

'Because I'm still finding it difficult to accept my place in your scheme of things,' she said. 'To have a child and leave it—what kind of person would I be if I found that easy?'

His face closed up again. 'That was the bargain.'

'Raine's, not mine.'

'No matter.' He stood up abruptly, depositing her back on her feet with scant ceremony. 'Your sister isn't here; your are. Leave me now. I wish to be alone.'

She left the room without looking back, her mind in turmoil. To go was the only sane solution, yet a part of her wanted equally desperately to stay. Somewhere inside that implacable exterior there existed a man she might even learn to like, given half a chance. Only there wasn't going to be any chance, was there? Felipe had no desire for her beyond that of any man for any woman, no need other than the one already stated. Once she had given him what he wanted from her, it would be finished.

She changed into a pair of jeans and a cotton shirt before lying down on the bed to rest until it was time to go, taking the precaution of setting the alarm on her digital wrist-watch for one a.m. first. The household was normally quiet by then, and it would give her seven whole hours before her absence was discovered when Yola brought her up her morning coffee. The stables might well be checked before then, but that was a chance she had to take. Twenty kilometres wasn't all that far. Once she reached Jerez, she could hire a taxi to take her to Seville.

Always providing she could find one in the middle of the night, came the thought, hastily shelved because it smacked of defeat before she had even got started. If not a taxi, then some other form of transport. Once away from this place, she was not coming back. Not for anything or anyone!

The bleeping of the alarm woke her from a sleep that had left her feeling far from rested. Not daring to put on a light, she rinsed her face and cleaned her teeth at the bathroom basin, and ran a comb hastily through her hair. Back in the bedroom, she slid her arms into the denim jacket, and slung the shoulder-bag crosswise over her chest. Her shoes were of the brogue type, and adequate for the job. She had hoped to do some walking, she recalled. It was only four days since her arrival. It scarcely seemed possible. She had been so guilelessly happy, so looking forward to her new job.

No point in dwelling on it, she told herself firmly. There was too much else to occupy her mind right now.

No sound reached her ears when she cautiously opened the door. Everything was in darkness. Careful to close the door behind her again, she made her way to the staircase. Her eyes had already adjusted, enabling her to step with relative confidence down the wide sweep.

The rubber soles of her shoes made little sound on the terrazzo surface of the hallway. Passing the study, she traversed the corridor that led through to the rear premises and the service door she had noted previously, praying that it would not be locked. It was, but the key was right there in the lock. Passing through, she locked it again, leaving the key on the outside.

It took only minutes to reach the stables. The animals were secured in individual loose-boxes, the tack-room situated at the far end of the row. Beyond that again lay store-rooms, and lastly the sleeping quarters of the stable-boy himself.

Jan had spent the better part of an hour the previous day cultivating the young man, drawing him out to discuss the relative merits of each of his beloved charges in order to discover which of them might prove the safest bet. Her final decision had come to rest on a chestnut mare named Santina, who was reputedly steady and tractable, and certainly seemed friendly enough. Jan trusted to luck that her horsemanship would be equal to the task of tacking up and clearing the stable without wakening Carlos.

Each of the saddles and bridles in the tack-room was labelled with the name of the horse to which it belonged. Finding Santina's tack was easy enough, carrying the heavy, ornately tooled leathers another matter altogether. The mare whickered softly when Jan eased open the door of her box, but made no move other than a quizzical turn of her head as the saddle was somehow heaved across her back and the girth tightened.

Breath coming hard, Jan paused for a moment before attempting the bridle, grateful when the animal accepted the bit without protest. So far, so good. All that remained was to tie the pieces of cloth she had brought with her about the hoofs in order to muffle the sound until she was far enough away, and then it was all systems go.

It had all taken much longer than she had anticipated, she realised, catching sight of the illuminated face of her watch. A quarter to two already, and she wasn't even clear of the estate! Unless she galloped the animal the whole way to town, which was hardly practical at night on a road she didn't even know, it was going to be coming up to dawn before she got there. That might make things easier in one way, but it vastly reduced the chances of her reaching Seville before her escape was discovered.

Felipe would guess which way she would have gone, of course. He might even attempt to cut her off. So supposing she made for Cádiz on the coast instead? she thought. Where there was sea, there were boats. Lacking a passport, she would be restricted to Spanish destinations, but if she could reach Barcelona, for instance, she would surely find help of some kind. An appeal to the Spanish authorities was still not beyond consideration. They would *have* to listen to her!

She led the mare from the stable vicinity before mounting, tentatively testing the animal's response to the rein. No problem there, she realised thankfully, as silken muscles obeyed her commands without hesitation. She might even risk the occasional canter on this horse.

The *hacienda* grounds themselves were separated from the vineyards by a high stone wall in which double ironwork gates provided entrance from the road. Jan managed to open one of them without dismounting, urging Santina through the gap, and pulling the gate closed again behind them. In moonlight, the whole countryside looked different, the massed vines stretching blackly to either hand. Not until they had covered a good half-mile did she stop to remove the cloths, patting the smooth neck in gratitude.

'You're a gem!' she told the animal, receiving an amiable nuzzle by way of reply.

Mounted again, she urged the mare into a trot, sticking to the grass verge where the going was softer. The whole thing had been so comparatively easy, there was almost a sense of anticlimax.

They had a long way to go yet, though, she reminded herself, and her muscles were already beginning to feel the strain. Riding was a sport one had to practise regularly to stay properly hardened to the saddle, and it had been almost a year since she was last up. By the time she reached Cádiz she was going to know about it, she concluded ruefully.

She knew about it long before that. Jeans were no real protection against the rubbing of stirrup leathers, she found. Walking the animal eased the situation a little, but also extended the journey time by a dangerous amount. She could only hope that Felipe would indeed assume she was making for Seville should her flight be discovered earlier than anticipated, and head in that direction himself. By the time he had ascertained his mistake, she would be on a ferry and out of harm's way. Let him try to find her then!

At this hour even the cicadas were resting, the silence broken only by the occasional cry of some animal, or the rustle of the night wind through the olive trees which were now lining the narrow roadway. The sound of an engine in the far distance was unmistakable.

Heart sinking, Jan urged her mount into a canter, no longer noticing the discomfort as fear overtook her. That the fast approaching vehicle was driven by Felipe she had little doubt. There was nowhere she could go to escape detection. No way she could outdistance a car either, but it wasn't going to stop her trying.

The fall had to be inevitable. She felt Santina stumble, and was the next moment sliding forwards over her neck to land with bruising force. Perhaps she passed out for a moment or two, because the next thing she knew was the heat and dampness of the animal's breath on the back of her neck. She hurt everywhere, but at least she could move all her limbs.

Pushing the mare aside, she attempted to sit up, gasping as pain creased her temple. She must have caught her head, she realised, although there didn't appear to be any blood.

The engine sound filled her ears. Even as she tried to force herself to her feet, the long, low-slung coupé drew to a screeching stop beside her.

Felipe was out of the car and towering over her before she could make any further move. Moonlight only served to emphasise the grim lines of his mouth and jaw.

'Stay still!' he commanded. 'You may have a fracture.'

'There's nothing broken.' Jan forced out the words through stiff lips, the bitter knowledge of defeat seeping deep into her bones. 'Nothing that need concern *you*, anyway.'

'I'll be the judge of that.' He drew her to her feet, turning her head with a hand hard under her chin, to push back the hair with the other hand and feel gently over her scalp. 'This bump needs attention.'

'Look to the mare first,' she said with scorn. 'She's worth more than I am!'

The hand still holding her brought her head back round to face him, the look in his eyes searing her very soul. 'Hold your tongue!' he gritted. 'How far did you hope to get, little fool?'

'Far enough to be free of you,' she spat back at him, relinquishing all hold on her rioting emotions. 'I've hated every moment of the time I've been forced to spend with you! Don't you understand that?'

The twist of his lips flicked every nerve in her body. 'That wasn't the impression you gave me yesterday evening.'

'So I'm a good actress. Your kind of egotism takes little convincing!' She wanted to wipe the smile from his face, to rake the smooth olive skin with her nails until she drew blood. One hand came up involuntarily to follow through on the urge, to be seized in a grip of iron and forced down again behind her back, bringing her body into closer proximity with his male hardness.

'My senses,' he said contemptuously, 'are neither dull nor dead. Last night you were mine for the taking. Your whole body yearned for my touch.'

It hurt all the more because it was so close to the truth, but she couldn't afford to let him see that. 'If I trembled at all, it was in disgust, not desire,' she claimed. 'I wanted to be sick!'

Fire leapt in the dark eyes. 'Then be sick now,' he grated.

The buttons of her shirt tore through the material as he ripped a hand down the front, the brevity of her brassière no barrier to the force of his intention. Jan felt the snap fastener at her back give way at the same time as the thin satin straps; the whole garment was jerked from her body and tossed aside. The fingers curving her breast were warm and supple, capturing the tautened peak of her nipple and bringing it up to meet the mouth he bent towards it. She clutched at his hair in a frenzy of sensation, her mouth opening on a silent scream at the sheer agony his tongue was inflicting on the throbbing flesh. There was no gentleness in him, just unremitting demand, hurting her yet rousing her at one and the same time.

His lips left her breast to move slowly up towards her throat, lingering on the vulnerable hollow at its base for interminable seconds before traversing the taut length to find her mouth. If there had been any rejection in her at all, Jan was past caring. She was aware of his own arousal, found her body adjusting automatically to accommodate the potent thrust of his hips. She wanted to be with him, a part of him, to feel the full power of his loins pressuring open her trembling thighs.

Her mouth grew feverish in its response to his kisses, lips moving blindly, yearningly, her naked breasts brushing the wall of his chest. Loosing one hand, he opened his shirt, drawing a faint moan to her lips at the electric thrill of his body hair against her nipples. She heard a voice saying his name, realising without surprise that it was her own. The panic and fear had receded to a distance where they no longer counted. Nothing counted except for this moment, this man, this overwhelming need for fulfilment.

It was Felipe himself who called the halt. His breathing was heavy and harsh, his jaw set rigidly as he thrust her away from him.

'It will not happen here in the fields, like peasants!' he stated grimly. 'Cover yourself. We return to the *hacienda*.'

Hands nerveless, Jan took the free ends of her shirt front and tied them together, folding the material across her breasts as best she could. Felipe had tucked his own shirt back into his trousers and was standing by the car when she lifted her head again. He looked remote, the severity of his features belying the passion he had displayed so few moments ago.

How could she have let herself be degraded in that way? she thought numbly. He had done this deliberately, just to show her who was master here. He had proved it, too, hadn't he? She was no more capable of staying aloof from him now than she apparently was of escape from his clutches. Which left her with little choice but to accept her lot.

Only never the whole of it, came the fierce resolve. If she bore his child, she would be taking it with her when she eventually went!

Dawn was beginning to break by the time they reached the *hacienda*. Felipe had unsaddled the mare and left her to make her way home at her own pace. Horse stealing was not a problem in this part of the world, Jan gathered.

Leaving the car parked at the foot of the double flight of marble steps leading to the main entrance, he took her up to her room and through into the bathroom, indicating that she should sit down while he found cotton wool and antiseptic.

The latter stung like fury when applied to the swelling under her hairline, bringing involuntary tears to her eyes. She blinked them away swiftly, hating to have him see her weakness.

'If you're feeling sick again,' he said with satire, 'I'll have you a potion prepared.'

'I'm all right,' she denied, and wondered if he really would have called one of the staff from their bed had she answered otherwise. Yet why not? They were here to serve, whatever the time of day or night.

'Later,' he went on, allowing the hair to fall back into place, 'I'll call for Dr Valdes to come and take a look at you.'

'It isn't necessary,' she protested. 'Really, I——'

'I'll decide what is necessary.' His tone was short. 'You'll go back to your bed now, and catch up on the sleep you missed.' He met her swift upward glance with a thin smile. 'You're safe enough from my attentions for now. I have need of sleep myself.'

The question was dragged from her as he turned to go. 'How did you find out I'd gone so soon?'

'That,' he said without change of expression, 'is something you will have to work out for yourself. You realise, of course, that I no longer feel bound by any promise I made you?'

Her voice was low. 'Yes.'

'That, at least, is something.'

Jan waited until she heard the outer door close behind him before stirring herself into movement. She wouldn't have been surprised if he had locked her in the room, but she had heard no key turn. No doubt he considered her too thoroughly demoralised to make any further attempt to leave.

He was right, too. Her spirits were at rock bottom. The fact that he could arouse such an unprecedented response in her was difficult to come to terms with. Had the secretarial position been genuine, it was doubtful if he would even have noticed her—not in any way that mattered. She would just have been another employee.

If nothing else, she had to retain her self-respect. To give in to the emotions he summoned so easily would be tantamount to condoning his purpose. Not that lack of response would stop her from getting pregnant, she concluded hollowly. She had no means at her disposal to do that. For the first time ever she regretted not being on the pill.

The sun was turning the world from grey to gold before she finally fell asleep. When she opened her eyes again, Dr Valdes was standing by the bed.

'I am sorry to waken you,' he apologised. 'Don Felipe was concerned that you sleep so long.'

'What time is it?' she asked, coming up on an elbow in momentary confusion before the pain from bruised muscles brought memory rushing in. Oh, hell, she thought, dropping her head back on the pillows again, what do I do?

'The time' said the doctor, 'is five minutes after one o'clock. How do you feel?'

Like death, she wanted to answer. 'My head aches,' she mumbled instead. 'I had a fall.'

'So I understand.' He sat down on the edge of the bed, reaching to part the hair above her temple and press gently around the site of the swelling. 'There appears to be no serious damage,' he proclaimed at length, after shining a light in each of her eyes. 'You were fortunate, *señorita*. Sleepwalking can sometimes have tragic results.'

Jan looked at him sharply, suspecting ridicule, but his expression held only professional solicitation. So Felipe himself must have supplied the lie. There could only be one reason for that. The doctor knew why she was here, of course, but was he aware that she was being held against her will?

She saw the movement out of the corner of her eye, turning her head as Felipe himself moved into closer proximity.

'We must take more care in future,' he said. 'I'll see you to your car.'

A summary dismissal, but the other man appeared to find nothing unusual in it. Jan threw back the covers as soon as they had left the room, and pressed herself up-

right, wincing a little at the soreness of her chafed thighs.
She must have been totally exhausted to have slept for
so many hours—emotionally as well as physically. She
felt little better for it now. Dr Valdes probably wouldn't
have helped her, even if she had managed to confide in
him. These people stuck together.

She was easing aching muscles in a warm bath when
Felipe strolled into the room. Snatching up the towel she
had draped ready over a stool, she clutched it in front
of her, eyes blazing blue fire at him as he paused just
inside the door.

'What do you think this is?' she demanded. 'A peep
show?'

'There's no part of your body that will remain un-
known to me before too long,' he returned, totally unmoved by her reaction. 'Last night I held in my hands
the breasts you're so intent on covering. Do you think
my eyes were closed then?'

Colour burned in her cheeks. 'That still gives you no
right to just walk in here like this!'

'I'm tired of telling you,' he said. 'I have the right to
do anything I wish.' He took another of the huge thick
towels from the nearby rail and shook it out, mounting
the two steps to hold it up to her. 'Come on out of there.'

What he might do if she refused, she wasn't sure, and
didn't care to find out. Coming slowly and awkwardly
to her feet, she dropped the wet towel and suffered him
to wrap the other around her, clutching it close as he
lifted her bodily from the bath.

'I can manage myself,' she gasped as he commenced
to rub her dry. 'Leave me alone!'

'But I've no wish to leave you alone,' he said on a
softer note, pausing to put his lips to her nape where the

hair had parted. 'I warned you there would be no more waiting. Let me take this away. I want to look at you.'

He would take it by force if necessary, she surmised. If she had to do it at all, she would do it with dignity. There was no other recourse left.

Allowing the towel to slide to the ground, she steeled herself to turn and face him—to stand still and straight under his appraisement. He took his time, his gaze sliding over breasts and slender waist to follow the curve of her hips down to the shadowed joining of her thighs. Her self-consciousness faded before the look growing in his eyes, replaced by a warmth that started in the very pit of her belly, and slowly expanded until it reached every extremity. Her limbs felt weak and shaky, her heartbeats so heavy that she could hear nothing else.

'You're very lovely,' he breathed. 'How much so, I wasn't fully aware.' He reached out a finger to lightly scoop the drop of moisture still clinging between her breasts, transferring it to his lips while he looked deep into her eyes. The smile was slow, sensual, stirring her innermost being. A tingling heat contracted her inner thighs. She drew in a quivering breath, tongue moistening, lips gone suddenly dry.

Lifting one unresisting hand, he slid her fingers inside his shirt, watching her face as she curled them instinctively to the wiry feel of his body hair. As he unfastened the rest of the buttons and slid the garment from his shoulders, she stood motionless, seeing the ripple of muscle beneath the smooth olive skin, sensing the latent power. This time he took both her hands and pressed them flat against his chest, his eyes glowing with an inner fire.

'Feel me,' he invited. 'Let your fingers explore me, *mi querida*, the way mine will explore you. There can be no secrets between us.'

'I can't.' Her voice was a whisper, scarcely audible even to herself above the wild beating of her heart.

'The male body is abhorrent to you?' he asked.

She shook her head. 'It's just that I was brought up to believe there should be some depth of feeling between two people first.'

'You've no feeling for *me* except hatred, if I'm to take your word. Yet you want me.' He put a finger to her lips as she opened them to speak, shaking his head with a hint of mockery in his eyes. 'Don't try to deny it. Even now your heart leaps to my touch.' The finger moved to trace the shape of her mouth with a slow sensitivity that parted her lips. 'I'll teach you how to pleasure me, *querida*, but only after you have learned what it is to know me. We have the whole afternoon at our disposal.'

Jan swallowed on the lump in her throat. It would be so easy to let herself drown in that voice of his, to give in to the craving that tormented her body. She wasn't truly a woman until she had known a man, that was what he was telling her. He was in all probability right, but was she prepared to pay the price he demanded for his initiation? Once submitted, neither body nor mind would ever be free of him again.

'If the child is all you want from me, none of this is necessary,' she said, her tone low but distinct. 'Why don't you just get it over?'

The hand he had allowed to follow her jawline fastened suddenly and violently in her hair, jerking back her head so that she looked straight into his leaping eyes. 'I'm not an animal! Why do you seek to anger me?'

'Because I'm not prepared to become your slave—in bed or out of it!' she retorted, taking refuge in an anger of her own. 'Whatever you want from me, you're going to have to take!'

For a long moment she really believed he was going to throw her to the floor and do just that. Only by degrees was the white-hot fury brought under control. When he finally spoke, it was in tones that were remarkably even.

'You'll not deprive me of the pleasure of making you eat your words. Before the day is out, you'll *beg* me to take you!'

CHAPTER FOUR

JAN went limp as he swung her up in his arms and carried her through to the bedroom. Laying her down on the bed, he stood back to unbuckle his belt, his eyes never leaving hers. She turned her head away as he undid the zip, her whole body trembling uncontrollably.

'Look at me,' he commanded a moment later. 'There's nothing shameful in the human body—male *or* female.' The mattress dipped as his weight came to bear on it, his hand seizing her chin and forcibly turning her face back towards him. 'I said look at me!'

She did so because she couldn't avoid it, the heat washing through her in one great wave. He had one knee bent on to the bed, the other leg stretched for support. His skin had a healthy gleam about it, the thick clustering of hair on his chest thinning down to a narrow V just below his waistline. Muscle ridged the flat stomach, repeated in the strength of his loins.

Reaching for her hand, he guided her to him, watching her face as he let himself down at her side. His arm came around her, the tapering fingers beginning a slow and infinitely tender pilgrimage down the contours of her body, sending ripple after ripple of melting sensation coursing through her.

Mouth dry, breath coming short and fast, Jan had no power over her limbs. He was leaving no part of her unexplored, no secret unlocked, his touch like a butterfly's wing across the fluttering skin of her belly, catching the breath in her throat as he found her most intimate self.

Hardly knowing what she was doing, she reached up and drew the dark head down to her breasts, her back arching instinctively to bring the soft fullness into greater prominence. Her hips began moving to his command, her whole being seized by the overwhelming need to find relief from the delicious, agonising torment he was inflicting on her. The cry that broke from her lips was torn from some place so deep, it ripped her throat.

'That is only the beginning,' he promised softly. He brought his body further over her, his weight supported by his arms as he looked down into her unguarded face. When he kissed her she responded blindly, parting her lips to his asking. He was scarcely touching her, his chest just brushing the tips of her nipples, driving her wild with frustrated desire for closer contact. Her fingers played over the sleek muscles of his back, nails digging crescents into the taut flesh.

'Not yet, little one,' he breathed mockingly. 'Not until you say the words I want to hear from you. "I beg you, Felipe." Let me hear you say it to me, *mi querida*!'

'I hate you!' she whispered fiercely, and saw the cruel mouth take on an added slant.

'But you want me, too. Is that not so?'

'No!' Desperation lent her voice strength. 'All I want is to be free of this whole sordid mess!'

'There's nothing sordid in two people making love,' he said. 'Tell me you want me, and I'll grant you the ease you crave.'

'Go to hell!' It was all she could do to force the words between her clenched teeth. 'Just go to hell!'

His laugh was a goad in itself. 'So much spirit, little tigress, but I've no intention of going anywhere without you.'

His knee came between hers, opening her thighs to the full, potent weight of him. She tensed involuntarily, breath suspended against the incursion she both feared and longed for, body quivering like an aspen leaf in a breeze. Gently, so very gently at first, he began to move, his lips feathering tiny kisses over her eyes and down the line of her cheekbone to cherish her mouth with a delicacy that stirred her soul. It was so different from everything she had ever imagined. So utterly, wonderfully different!

There was pain in the end, but not for long, the memory of it vanishing along with the last of her reservations as he joined his body wholly to hers and carried her into another world.

He made no immediate attempt to leave her afterwards. Held close in his arms, Jan felt such a sense of peace and contentment, she wanted to weep.

'Rest,' he commanded softly when she stirred. 'We have all the time in the world.'

She must have slept for a while, awakening to find herself lying between the silk sheets. Heaviness settled about her heart at the realisation that she was alone again.

But why would he have stayed with her? she asked herself dully. As far as he was concerned, this had simply been a necessary first stage—one he was no doubt immensely relieved to have done with. She should feel fortunate that he had taken the time and trouble to make the occasion as painless as possible for her.

Though painless hardly did justice to the experience, she acknowledged, recalling the sheer ecstasy of those final, tumultuous moments. Felipe de Rimados was no animal, indeed. She had felt so close to him while he had held her—not just in the physical sense, but all the way through. She mustn't allow her emotions to become involved, she thought in desperation, burying her face in the pillow. That way lay heartache of a kind she would never overcome.

It took the sound of running water to penetrate her consciousness. Rolling over, she saw the clothing Felipe had discarded still strewn on the floor. So he hadn't walked out on her, after all! He was right there in the bathroom, taking a shower. Relief flooded through her. It made no difference to the overall situation, but at least he wasn't treating her like some brief encounter.

She was sitting hugging her knees through the sheet when he eventually emerged. A towel slung low about his hips was his only covering—and not a large one at that.

'You can still blush to see me?' he queried with amusement as he moved towards the bed. 'Then I still have much to teach you. But first I've run you a warm and soothing bath to ease your bruises.'

'I don't have any—' she began, then winced as she attempted to straighten out her legs. 'I forgot about my saddle sores,' she acknowledged ruefully.

'I take that as a compliment,' he said. 'You were certainly not inhibited by them a little while ago.' He paused at the foot of the bed, brows lifting when she made no move. 'You'd prefer I carried you again?'

If the alternative was walking naked across the room under his gaze, the answer was yes, she thought wryly. It was all very well for him to talk about teaching her to view nudity in the same way he so obviously did himself, but agreeing in practice was an entirely different thing. She couldn't bring herself to throw back the only covering she had.

'Come.' His tone had gentled. Taking the bottom of her sheet in his hand, he gently drew it down and away from her. 'You're beautiful. Too beautiful to hide yourself away from my eyes. I know every inch of those lovely silken curves. There's nothing left of which to be protective.'

'Becoming uninhibited isn't an overnight affair,' she responded. 'I'm not used to being this way with any man.'

His mouth thinned a fraction. 'I'm not *any* man!'

She sighed. 'I didn't mean it quite like that.'

There was a slight pause before he inclined his head. 'I don't pretend to appreciate all the nuances of your language. The water will soon be too cool.'

It took an effort still, but she made herself move from the bed. Her back felt vulnerable, her movements were jerky, stiff with self-consciousness. She had half anticipated he would follow her, but he stayed where he was.

'This time I'll allow you to bathe uninterrupted,' he said, as if reading her mind. 'I'll be here when you're finished.'

Her stomach muscles contracted. He wasn't through with her yet. I will teach you to pleasure me, he had said. She had only the vaguest idea of what that actually meant.

It was a relief to reach the comparative privacy of the bathroom, to close the door and stand for a moment gathering herself together. The surrounding mirrors reflected a face and figure that looked familiar. It was only inside that she felt different, the lingering, pleasurable ache so new.

She was truly a woman now. 'Deflowered', as Felipe had termed the event. She felt her senses stir afresh at the memory of that joining, the muscles of her inner thighs go into sudden spasm. She wanted him again, she realised, the intensity of the need growing with each breath she drew. The sooner she took the bath he had run for her, the sooner she could be with him again.

The water was just lukewarm, the fragrance rising from it tantalising her nostrils. Felipe must have ladled in salts from one of the glass jars. Freesia, the perfume reminded her of. Lying full length, she closed her eyes for a moment, visualising the lean body, shoulders so broad and strong, tapering down to that narrow waist and hard male hip, the proud manhood. Her lips formed his name, cherishing the shape of it, the feel of it. Felipe de Rimados, the only man in the world she——

Recollection was sudden and soul-destroying. That man out there had no feeling for her. All he wanted was to impregnate her with his seed. It was even possible he had already done so.

The yearning had vanished, replaced by a pain she could hardly bear. How could she feel anything for someone who would do what he was intent on doing? A man who would readily have used force if it had proved necessary. Only it hadn't been necessary, had it? She had given herself to him with barely a token protest. How amused he must have been at the ease of his conquest. He was probably congratulating himself even now.

It might already be too late to escape the consequences of that possession. Even if by chance he hadn't fulfilled his intention yet, he eventually would. Only when she was certified with child might he leave her alone.

She lingered as long as she dared before nerving herself
to return to the bedroom, a towelling robe belted tightly
about her waist. Her emotions on finding him fully
dressed again were too confused to be sorted.

'I have to go out,' he said. 'Some problem at one of
the *bodegas*.' His regard narrowed a little as he viewed
her. 'You have something you wish to say to me?'

Jan shook her head, her throat as tight as a drum.
She stiffened as he moved towards her, nerving herself
not to move when he slid a hand behind her nape and
tilted her head to his mouth. In spite of everything, the
kiss stirred her. It was all she could do to stay quiescent
under it. There was an odd look in his eyes when he
finally drew away.

'Tonight,' he said with a certain deliberation, 'you
share *my* bed. Yola will bring you tea in a little while.'

He went without bothering to wait for an answer. Not,
Jan acknowledged, that there was anything she could
have found to say. Obviously a member of the staff must
have passed on the message, which meant that the whole
household probably knew what had been taking place
here in her bedroom this afternoon. How did she face
any of them again with that thought hanging over her?

It was still only a little after four o'clock, she realised
with a sense of shock. A lifetime seemed to have passed
since she had woken to find Dr Valdes standing over her.
In another few hours Felipe would take her again. Pro-
tests now would be treated with disdain. Pregnant or
not, she had to escape him, she thought despairingly.
There had to be *some* way!

She made sure she was dressed by the time Yola
brought the promised tea. As usual there was little to be
gleaned from the girl's expression, but Jan was desperate enough to ignore her reticence for once.

'Don't go,' she appealed. 'I want to talk to you.'

A watchful look sprang in the other eyes. 'I have duties, *señorita*.'

'Nothing that can't wait a while.' Jan held her gaze. 'You know why I'm here, Yola?'

There was hesitation before her head slowly inclined. 'You are to become the mother of Don Felipe's child.'

'But not by my own choice. I'm being held here against my will.' Jan searched for some sign of empathy in her face. 'Do you think that's right?'

'It is not for me to say, *señorita*.' Her tone was wooden. 'I know only what I am told.'

'But it's true! I'm a prisoner. I tried to escape last night, but I was brought back.'

'You stole Santina. Carlos is to be replaced because he allowed this to happen.' The mask had dropped just a little. 'No one in Andalucia will give him another job when it becomes known that Don Felipe no longer trusts him.'

'But that's unfair.' Jan was driven to forget her own problems for the moment. 'He wasn't to blame! I took every precaution to ensure he wouldn't hear anything.'

Yola's gesture said it all. The master's decree was not to be argued with. Well, *she* could argue with it, thought Jan determinedly. Felipe had to be made to see the utter injustice of his action. Carlos should not have to suffer because of her.

'I'll speak to Don Felipe about it,' she said, and added recklessly, 'Tell Carlos his job will be safe. I promise him.'

Yola looked unconvinced, but she nodded. 'I will tell him.'

Any further appeal on her own behalf was going to be unfruitful, Jan realised. The girl was hardly going to jeopardise both her own and her father's positions. Felipe ruled with an iron hand; she supposed she should feel fortunate that he had chosen to don the velvet glove where she was concerned, otherwise her initiation into the mysteries of womanhood might have been very different.

Despite the glorious sunshine outside, she spent the rest of the daylight hours in her room, preparing herself both mentally and physically for the coming reunion. At eight-thirty, dressed in the classic black silk that was the pride of her wardrobe, she made her way down to the *salón*.

Don Felipe would not be returning for dinner, Juan informed her. She was to eat alone. Seated in isolation at the vast table, Jan felt as if she had been slapped in the face. Yet what else might she have expected? she asked herself. Felipe was hardly going to rush his affairs for her sake. He had taken his fill of her earlier; perhaps he'd even decided that enough was enough for the time being. Her responses to his efforts could have provided little stimulation.

So hopefully she would sleep alone tonight, she thought, trying to ignore the hollow feeling deep down inside. And every other night, too. In a little over two weeks she would know whether she was pregnant or not. It was going to be the longest fortnight of her life.

By ten o'clock, with the lonely meal over, she could stand the atmosphere indoors no longer. The inner courtyard provided little more air. She finished up out at the pool, relishing the light breeze that brought the mingled scents of lemon and jasmine to her nostrils.

Faintly and tantalisingly, she could hear the sound of music. Coming from the belt of trees just beyond the formal area of gardens, she judged. Gypsies, perhaps.

Andalucia was, by all accounts, one of the few areas of the country where they still roamed the highways and byways in travelling bands. If they were there at all, it had to be with permission. Otherwise they were hardly going to make their presence known the way they were doing.

The urge to go and see grew in her by the minute. Apart from a good book, or the television, there was little other entertainment on offer. She could reach the spot via one of the paths radiating out from the other side of the pool, she believed.

The sandals she was wearing were hardly suited to walking on grass, as she found when she emerged from the shrubbery into open ground. After a moment or two, she took them off and continued in her bare feet, liking the springy feel of the turf beneath her toes.

The music grew louder as she approached the trees. She could see the flickering light from a fire between the trunks. As far as she knew, no one was following her— a lapse someone would no doubt pay for should she seize the opportunity to make another attempt to escape. If these people could be persuaded to hide her in one of their vans, she might even succeed this time.

Hope faded as swiftly as it had arisen. The gypsy encampment would probably be the first place searched should she just disappear. She had to be more subtle than that.

Occupying a sizeable clearing, the encampment itself was composed of some half a dozen colourful wagons. The horses were tethered close by where Jan paused to take stock, just within the shelter of the trees. She took care not to spook them with a careless movement.

Firelight playing over taut-skinned olive faces, the whole scene was exactly as her imagination had painted it. One of the men was playing a guitar, the sound plaintive and discordant to her untutored ear. Over by the fire, a young girl of no more than twelve or thirteen years of age performed the series of stylised movements recognisable even to Jan as flamenco, urged on by the smiles and calls of those about her.

Easing her position, Jan trod an unwary foot on a dry twig, snapping it with a noise that, even to her own ears, sounded loud enough to penetrate the dullest sense. A whinny from one of the horses set the others moving restlessly, as though they sensed her presence, if unable as yet to scent it.

'Who are you?' asked a voice at her back, and she whirled to confront the man whose approach she hadn't even been aware of. Short and stocky in build, his bolero jacket heavily embroidered over a full-sleeved scarlet shirt, he was nevertheless a figure of command. The firelight glinted on swarthy features and suspicious eyes.

'I heard the music from the house,' she explained hesitantly. 'I'm sorry if I seemed to be spying on you.'

The suspicion was replaced by some other expression less easily defined. 'You are the guest of Don Felipe?'

'Yes.'

His bow was polite. 'Then we shall be honoured if you will join us.'

Already regretting the impulse that had brought her here, Jan hesitated. To refuse might be to offer deadly insult, yet she dreaded the prospect of stepping out of her hiding-place into view of so many curious eyes.

'I should be getting back,' she said weakly.

He dismissed the protest with a sweep of his hand. 'You must first allow us to show you our hospitality.'

All talking stopped as they emerged from the shadows. Still carrying her sandals in one hand, Jan felt small and

somehow defenceless under the concerted stares. The
man at her side drew her into the midst of the gathering,
procuring a seat for her with the flick of a finger.

'Bring food and drink for our guest,' he commanded.
'Play, José. It is the music that drew her to us.'

'My name is Jan Presley,' she offered diffidently as
the guitarist obliged. 'I mustn't stay long. Don Felipe
will be wondering where I got to.'

'You are the one who is to bear Don Felipe's child.'
It was one of the women who spoke, and it wasn't a
question.

Jan looked at her sharply. 'How do you know that?'

'It matters little how I know,' said the other. She
moved forward to take a seat at Jan's side on the fallen
log, reaching for her hand. 'Let me see your lines.'

Jan resisted with effort the urge to snatch her hand
back. Gypsies were into fortune telling the world over,
it seemed. Obviously they had learned of her presence
in the Rimados household—and reason for it—from one
of the servants. There would be little else they could know
about her.

The hand holding her wrist belonged to a woman of
indeterminate years. She could, Jan reckoned, have been
anywhere between forty and sixty. Her eyes had endless
depth. Looking into them brought an odd sensation
almost like vertigo.

Her fingers resting lightly on the ends of Jan's in order
to straighten out the palm, the fortune teller studied the
lines revealed. 'The child will be a son,' she stated quietly.
'He will be followed by another, and then a daughter.
Your life will be long, as that of Don Felipe himself is
to be. The way will not be smooth in the beginning, but
you will find contentment in the end.'

So much for precognition, thought Jan cynically. Felipe was interested in acquiring only the one son, not a whole family—and certainly not a life partner!

'You're saying I'll never return to my own country?' she asked with scepticism, and saw a faint smile cross the other face.

'You may return, but your heart will be here. You must follow your heart.'

Removing her hand abruptly from the suddenly unresisting grasp, Jan got to her feet. 'Thank you for the hospitality,' she said, 'but I have to go now. I shouldn't have come in the first place.'

'No, you should not.' Felipe spoke in English, moving into the firelight through the gap suddenly opened to him. The skin was drawn taut over the bones of his face, his whole manner one of controlled anger. 'You'll return with me now!'

Short of openly defying him, she had little choice but to obey. The fingers seizing hold of her arm were bars of pure steel. No one said a word as he led her away from the group towards the trees. Only when they were within the shadows and hidden from view did he pause to say coldly, 'Put on your shoes. You are not a gypsy!'

'I only took them off because it was difficult to walk over the grass in them,' she said. 'If we're going back this way, I'm going to have the same difficulty.'

'No matter. You'll put them on.'

'All right.' She suited her actions to her words, feeling the soft ground give beneath her heels as she brought her weight to bear. 'Just don't be too surprised if I fall flat on my face!'

'You won't fall.' Even in the near darkness, it was possible to see the glitter in his eyes. 'If you were hoping to gain help of some kind from our friends back there,

you would have been disappointed. They wouldn't risk
my displeasure.'

Not for anything, Jan decided, was she going to be
intimidated by his attitude. 'You mean they're afraid of
you?' she suggested silkily.

'I said nothing of fear.' His lip had curled. 'They are
on my land with my permission. Should I withdraw it,
they would be forced to move on.'

'They weren't here last night.'

'They come and they go.' He shook his head impatiently. 'It matters little why and when they came. You
had no business there.'

'I heard the music,' she said. 'With little else to do,
I thought I'd just take a look, that's all.' Her head was
up, her eyes challenging. 'Am I expected to just sit
around waiting for your return?'

'Yes,' he said. 'You're expected to do just that.'

'Then, tough!'

Hands like twin vices came down on her shoulders.
His voice was low, but no less of a threat. 'What is it
you dare say to me?'

'I said "tough",' she flashed back, refusing to retreat.
'I may have been forced into accepting certain aspects
of this situation, but that's as far as it goes. So if you're
planning on beating me, get on with it. Only I can assure
you, it isn't going to make me any other but what I am!'

For a timeless moment he continued to gaze at her,
his expression undergoing a slow but subtle alteration.
When he answered, it was on a note of reluctant admiration. 'Your spirit is indefatigable. Beating you would
afford me satisfaction, but serve little practical purpose,
I think. You'll give me your word that you won't attempt to visit the encampment again.'

It was a command, not a request, but the fury that had carried her this far was already fading, replaced by an emotion she didn't want to examine too closely. 'I suppose so.'

'That's no answer.'

'All right, then—yes.' There was a pause. It was in a final, feeble effort to get through that hide of his that she added softly, 'Been visiting one of your other women this evening, have you?'

His nostrils pinched. 'I take no other woman while I have you.'

'You don't have *me*,' she returned with emphasis. 'Only my body.'

'Then I must make the most of that,' he stated on a note of deliberation. 'We will walk slowly and conserve your energy. You'll be in need of it tonight.'

Her reaction to the promise was not wholly one of trepidation, acknowledged Jan ruefully as he urged her into motion with a hand hard at her waist. The memory of his lovemaking was too fresh in her mind. Tonight, no doubt, he would make her respond to him again; he was too practised in the art to fail. What she had to do was stay emotionally aloof. Only that way could she retain some measure of control over her life.

'How did you know where to look for me?' she asked after a moment or two, trying to sound matter-of-fact about it.

'Juan had you watched,' came the answer. 'In accordance with my instructions. He was about to despatch Manolo to bring you back when I returned.'

'If you hadn't been gone so long,' she couldn't resist pointing out, 'I wouldn't have had the opportunity to go wandering off. I trust the problem was resolved?'

'Eventually.' He made no effort to add to that bare statement. 'In future, I'll make certain you're fully entertained in my absence.'

She cast a swift sideways glance at the proud profile. 'Does that mean you're going to be away quite a lot of the time?'

'No more than necessary.' The mockery was edged. 'The times when my actual presence is essential are few and far between—in business, at least. My people have been with me for many years. They're to be trusted.'

The opening was too good to miss, although this was perhaps not the ideal time to make the plea. 'I think you're being a little unfair blaming Carlos for what I did last night,' she said with what diplomacy she could muster. 'If he loses his job because of it, I'm going to feel totally at fault.'

'So you are,' he returned.

There was little encouragement in his tone of voice, but her promise to Yola couldn't be put aside so easily. 'In that case, why blame Carlos at all?'

'Because it's his job to be aware of everything that happens at the stable.'

'He's surely allowed to sleep?'

Felipe paused in his stride, his face set in lines she recognised only too well. 'He asked you to intervene for him?'

Knowing she might have no further opportunity, she stood her ground. 'No, I haven't seen him. Yola told me he was to go.' The pause was brief, her voice entreating. 'Please, Felipe, will you reconsider? He'll never get another job if you turn him away!'

His mouth twisted. 'You plead so movingly!'

'Only because I feel so strongly about it. I'll *beg* you if it will make any difference,' she added, abandoning restraint. 'On my knees, if necessary!'

Faint though it was, the glint of humour in his eyes was encouraging. 'Such extremes should be reserved against greater need,' he advised drily. 'There may come a time when you have some favour to ask on your own behalf.'

'The only favour I'm likely to ask, you've already refused to consider,' she responded with intent. She hesitated before making the ultimate offer. 'If I give you my word not to try running away again, will you let Carlos stay in your employ?'

Regard suddenly narrowed, he took his time answering. When he did speak, it was on a flat, unemotional note. 'You would do this for a man you scarcely know?'

'It's a matter of principle,' she acknowledged. 'I don't have any choice.' She searched the strong features for some sign, half hoping he would refuse and let her off the hook she had forged for herself. 'Well?'

'He may stay.' There was still no measurable inflection. 'While you keep your word to me.'

Jan fell into step beside him as he turned abruptly towards the lights again, heart leaden. She had won, but at what cost? He was totally without mercy—for her or anyone else. To stay with him voluntarily meant to accept everything he had planned. And how could she possibly reconcile herself to *that* when the time came?

It was after eleven by the time they reached the *casa*. Felipe made no attempt to linger. At the head of the staircase he took her arm, turning her in the opposite direction to her own room.

'You move in with me,' he declared.

'I don't have a nightdress,' she protested feebly, and saw his lips slant a little.

'You will have no need of it—tonight or any other night. I want to feel you close to me.'

With the drumbeats so loud in her ears, Jan could find nothing to say. There was nothing she *could* say that was going to change anything. He had her bound hand and foot.

His bedroom was enormous, the bed itself more than six feet in width. Unlike the rest of the house, the furnishings in here were of a clean and modern design, executed in a wood not unlike teak in its grain and colour.

'Imported from Denmark,' Felipe explained, accurately assessing her thoughts as she glanced around. 'I prefer simplicity in my private quarters.'

He was loosening his tie as he spoke, fingers releasing the top button of the cream silk shirt. The jacket of his darker fawn suit he slung carelessly across a chair, tugging free the bottom of his shirt as he turned his head to look back to where she still stood just within the doorway.

'The bathroom is through there,' he said, indicating one of the two other doors in the far wall. 'You would like first use of it?'

She shook her head, hardly trusting her voice. The intimacy of this arrangement was going to be harder than ever to take. In every sense but the essential one, they would be living as man and wife.

'I'll wait,' she managed.

Whatever his reactions, he was keeping them to himself. 'As you prefer.'

She forced herself to move after he'd disappeared through the far door, taking in the fact that someone had already turned down the bedclothes in readiness for the night. If it wasn't known now that she was to share this room, it would be by morning. Yet what difference could it make to her position in the household? They were all only too well aware of her function.

In spite of everything, she found her senses stirred by the thought of what was to come. If the first time had been so wonderful, how would the second and third and fourth be? If she could only dissociate herself from the knowledge of what was eventually to happen; if there were only some way of ensuring she didn't become pregnant in the first place. When it came down to it, she knew so comparatively little about the workings of her own body.

Felipe was the knowledgeable one. Women were no mystery to him. To a certain extent, one might even say that familiarity had bred contempt. She was here for a purpose. Once that purpose had been fulfilled, he would discard her without a second thought.

Without realising it, she had come to a halt in front of the cheval-glass. Gazing at her shadowed reflection, she knew a renewal of determination. It would be up to her to fight for her rights if and when that time came. No child of hers was going to be abandoned. Not for all the money in the world!

Felipe was wearing a short towelling robe when he emerged from the bathroom. His hair was still slightly damp from the shower, Jan noted, his jawline smooth. He eyed her quizzically when she failed to get up from the chair where she had seated herself to wait for him.

'It is, as you would say, all yours,' he invited. 'My patience will stand fifteen minutes, no more. Any longer than that, and I'll come to fetch you to bed!'

'Didn't anyone ever tell you,' she said, getting to her feet, 'that anticipation is often the better part of the event?'

There was a flicker of surprise in his eyes, followed by a genuine amusement. 'No one that I can recall. But then, I've never before known anyone capable of producing such a remark. Anticipation, *querida*, is only a small part of the event. I look forward to proving that much to you.'

Safely inside the bathroom, with the door closed between them, she tried to steady her nerves. She could fight her responses, but what good was it going to do? He was hardly going to be deterred now.

If she were honest with herself, she wanted his lovemaking. Her whole body trembled at the memory of it. If it was inevitable anyway, why not make the most of it?

Because there was danger of losing far more than mere self-respect, came the answer. Felipe de Rimados was both ruthless and calculating, but there were facets to his character that could touch her innermost being. To allow herself to become embroiled would not only be foolish, it would be futile.

She stretched out her shower as long as she dared, only too well aware that Felipe wouldn't hesitate to keep his promise. Only when she was out and dried did she remember her lack of nightwear. A towel would have served as a wrap, but where was the point? she asked herself. He would only tell her to take it off. She could retain at least some initiative by forestalling him in that.

Apart from the soft glow of the bedside lamps, the room was in darkness when she at last emerged. Felipe was already in bed, his chest and shoulders bare above the single sheet covering the lower half of his body. His eyes smouldered as he watched her move towards him, his arousal instant and unmistakable. Throwing back the sheet, he drew her down to his side, his lips claiming hers with a passion that drove all rational thought from her mind.

It was a night Jan was to remember for the rest of her life—a night when she relinquished the last remnants of her girlhood along with her reserve.

Making love was a two-way affair, she discovered. There was as much pleasure to be found in giving as in receiving. Her shyness in following Felipe's initial guidance soon gave way to warm delight at the realisation of her own power to provide. To see his face contort, to hear his breath drawn sharply between his teeth, to feel his response to her caresses—it was sheer, heady jubilation. When she slept at last, it was the sleep of utter contentment.

He was still at her side when she opened her eyes again just after dawn. Lying on his back, with the thin sheet draped across his hips, he looked, she thought, like some pagan god!

Reaching out a hand, she trailed delicate fingertips down over his shoulder and one outflung arm, feeling the skin so smooth and warm over hard muscle. She knew the whole of him now—the way he knew her. Even in her wildest dreams, she had never come close to imagining the reality of it. Not that it changed anything. Much as Felipe appeared to enjoy making love to her, as far as he was concerned she was simply the means by which he would secure the continuance of his line.

'Why did you stop?' he asked softly, startling her because she hadn't known he was awake. He turned on to his side, putting out an arm to draw her closer, his hand sliding over her hip-bone with a possessiveness that thrilled her. 'Hold me,' he said. 'I want to feel your hands on me again.'

His lips sought hers, robbing her of any will she had left as he lifted her back to the heights.

CHAPTER FIVE

WHEN she opened her eyes again she was alone in the wide bed. Sunlight was pouring through the windows, wide beams dancing with dust mites.

According to the clock on the bedside table, it was only just after seven. Where Felipe might have gone at this hour, she had no idea. The only thing that mattered was that he *was* gone.

Rolling on to her back, she lay gazing at the figured ceiling while her mind roved over the past hours. Her mouth felt tender and a little swollen, her breasts sensitive to touch. Ravished was the word, she thought. Well and truly debauched. Not that she could bring herself to regret that part of it. If nothing else, she had given him satisfaction. More, she believed, than he had anticipated. His final kiss before they slept had held a certain tenderness—or so she liked to believe.

She was doing herself no good at all dreaming, she conceded hollowly. It was time to get up. Only as she came upright did she remember her lack of clothing. 'You move in with me,' Felipe had said, but that didn't help her right now when all her things were on the other side of the house.

It would either have to be the robe he had worn himself last night, or the black dress she had left on the bathroom floor—at least until she had verified his meaning. Perhaps he had only been referring to last night.

The warm shower revitalised her. She took the chance to wash her hair while she was under it, using one of the shampoos ranged along the rear shelf. Rubbed almost dry, it needed only a few strokes of one of the silver-backed brushes to smooth it into perfect shape.

She made sure there were no blonde hairs left among the bristles before replacing the brush where she had found it. She had always somehow imagined that Spanish men used brilliantine on their hair, but Felipe certainly didn't. His was thick and crisp and wonderful to run one's fingers through.

Yola brought in a breakfast-tray bare moments after she emerged from the bathroom. The girl's whole attitude was altered this morning, her smile warm and spontaneous.

'Carlos is to stay,' she said. 'He is very grateful, señorita, for all that you have done.'

'Considering it was me who brought the trouble on him in the first place, he has nothing to be grateful about,' Jan returned.

'There are many who would not have cared about his troubles,' came the swift reply. 'If there is anything you need, señorita, you have only to ask.'

Too late, Jan reflected wryly. The time for escape was past and gone. 'Don Felipe has left?' she asked.

'He has gone to Seville,' Yola confirmed. 'He will be back, he said, before dinner.'

A whole day to get through before she saw him again, thought Jan dully when she was alone. Was this to be the pattern of her life from now on?

How would Raine have handled the situation? she wondered. Could she really have walked away from it all when it came right down to it? To have agreed to the arrangement in the first place was some indication, she supposed. Raine had never worried overmuch about right or wrong, just so long as she came out on top. Marriage to a man in Alan Lester's financial position had to be a better deal than the one she had so neatly handed over—especially when she could pocket a cool five thousand pounds into the bargain.

It just went to show, she concluded ruefully, how little she had really known about her stepsister. Not that any of it mattered right now, anyway. She was in this on her own.

The room had a balcony reached via double glass doors. She took her coffee and croissants out there, relishing the morning freshness. The landscape beyond the estate was gentle and golden, the sierras a dramatic backdrop against the clear blue skies.

Just beyond those mountains lay the coastal regions frequented by the thousands of holiday-makers who journeyed to Spain every year. Jan had been to Marbella herself, yet had never ventured far inland. It was a whole other world, little changed, she imagined, over the years. Felipe himself was a traditionalist of the first water— where women were concerned, at any rate.

He already had English blood in his veins, he had told her. She wondered from how far back. The Rimados history might be worth delving into. If nothing else, it would occupy her mind.

The morning passed slowly. She took a swim after lunch, lying in the sun until the heat got too much for her. Unlike many fair-skinned people, she rarely went red before turning brown. Already her tan was beginning to show.

It was pleasant under the shade of the huge umbrella Manolo had erected for her. The elderly Spaniard seemed to be general dogsbody about the place, but he was always unfailingly good-humoured. He lived in the village, Jan had managed to discover, commuting to work every day on an ancient bicycle that was his pride and joy. His wife and all four of their sons were also employed on the estate.

The village itself had been built by Felipe's fore-bears—that much she had learned from Juan over lunch. The houses were rent-free and maintained by the estate, with each family allotted a plot of land on which to grow their own produce for the table. Autocrat or not, Felipe obviously cared for the welfare of his employees.

Lulled by the sultry heat and silence of the afternoon, she eventually drifted off to sleep, awakening again in confusion from a dream that faded even as she opened her eyes. Someone had tilted the umbrella to allow for the movement of the sun, she realised. Manolo, perhaps? Only when she turned her head did she see Felipe sitting just within the circle of shadow, watching her.

'I didn't hear the car!' she exclaimed, bringing the lounger into a more upright position with pressure on the leg rest. 'How long have you been back?'

'Some thirty minutes,' he said.

'You've been sitting there for half an hour?'

A smile briefly touched his lips. 'Perhaps not quite all of it. You needn't concern yourself. I took no liberties.'

She flushed a little. 'It hadn't occurred to me that you might.'

'Then it's the thought of being observed while you sleep that's troubling you?'

He had hit the nail on the head, although she couldn't have explained why it mattered so much to her. Vulner-ability, perhaps. 'It isn't important,' she said dismiss-ively. 'Did you go to Seville?'

'Yes.' There was an odd note in his voice. 'I had ar-rangements to make.' He paused, seeming to search for the words he wanted. 'I've done you a great wrong,' he stated. 'I make no excuses for it, because there are none that would suffice. There is only one way in which I can amend the situation. The marriage will take place in three days' time.'

She was too stunned to make any immediate comment. When she did find her voice, it seemed to be coming from a long way off. 'Won't that make things more difficult when the time comes to throw me out?'

'That isn't what I meant,' he said. 'The marriage will be permanent and binding.'

Jan stared at him, her mind spinning. 'What made you change your plans?' she whispered.

A muscle contracted at the corner of his mouth. 'The realisation of what I'd become. There are more honourable ways of ensuring the continuance of the Rimados line.'

Her heart slowed its beat again. Reparation, nothing else, she thought numbly. For a brief mad moment she had allowed herself to hope for some more meaningful reason. Why he should suddenly be taken by conscience, she couldn't begin to guess.

'One small item you seem to have forgotten,' she heard herself saying. 'What makes you think *I'm* prepared to make a permanent marriage?'

'The fact that there's every chance you're already carrying our child,' he returned levelly. 'Your stepsister was a different proposition. My judgement was at fault only where you're concerned.' He lifted his shoulders, expression wry. 'As I said, there are no excuses for the way I've treated you. I can only try to make up for it. At the very least, we're not indifferent to each other.'

'What about love?' It took everything she had to get the words out.

'An overrated emotion at best.'

'Not to me!'

'How can you know,' came the rejoinder, 'when, by your own admittance, you've never been in love?' He shook his head. 'You're looking for something that doesn't exist. All over the world people say "I love you", when what they really mean is "I want you". I want *you*, Janita, as the mother of my son.'

The Spanish interpretation of her name sounded soft on his lips. She swallowed. 'We could wait and see if I actually am pregnant before making any lasting decisions.'

'It's too late for that,' he stated. 'I already set matters into motion. The marriage will be sanctified here in our own church at Alagueda.'

She said huskily, 'You don't seem to have left me very much choice.'

'I had no intention of leaving you any choice. Naturally,' he added, 'you'll be sleeping alone now, until we are man and wife.'

'Isn't that rather like closing the stable door after the horse has bolted?' she asked on a note that elicited a sudden quizzical expression.

'If I take that to mean you'll find the parting as much of a strain as I shall myself, then I'm gratified. It is, however, a sacrifice I'm prepared to make.' His voice briskened. 'It will be a private ceremony, although my people here will no doubt wish to celebrate the occasion. Juan will organise everything. You have nothing to concern yourself with.' He added firmly, 'I think it time you went indoors now, out of the heat.'

Jan accompanied him without a murmur. Her mind felt quite unable to cope as yet. In the space of ten minutes her future had taken a whole new turning. Felipe's wife. Not even in her wildest dreams had she got as far as that. The reasons for this volte-face were clear enough, she supposed. Conscience could catch up with even the most hardened.

The gypsy woman last night had predicted a long life for the two of them together. Could there really be something in this fortune telling after all, or had it just been a stab in the dark? 'The way will not be smooth,' she had said. That much Jan could well believe. She might know Felipe's body, but his mind was still virtually a closed book. How could a marriage based on such scanty foundations ever hope to succeed?

'I'd better go up and change,' she said when they reached the coolness of the house, avoiding his eyes.

He made no attempt to touch her. 'I have some matters to attend to myself,' he agreed. 'Tonight we'll dine in Jerez and watch the flamenco. You must begin to appreciate our culture.'

The quietness of her room in no way helped to clear her mind. She felt isolated. No matter what she felt or didn't feel for Felipe, could she bear to live her life with a man who not only didn't love her, but denied that such an emotion even existed? If she were already carrying his child, then she might indeed have little choice . . . but if she weren't?

She was going around in circles, she acknowledged at that point. In three days' time Felipe de Rimados would be her husband; it would be too soon to be sure of her actual condition. Short of taking the risk and running out on him—which had already proved difficult—she had but one recourse, and that was to accept the situation as it stood.

Jerez itself, or what she could see of it by night, was pleasant and spacious. From outside, the restaurant where they were to eat looked like a private house. It wasn't a place open to the ordinary tourist, Felipe confirmed when they were seated at one of the intimately lit tables circling a raised area of floor.

Most of the other tables were already occupied, Jan noted. The women were beautifully dressed, making her very much aware of her own lack of sophistication in the lemon silk she had worn on her very first evening in Andalucia. If one went by colouring alone, she was not the only foreigner present tonight. Here and there were glimpses of hair as light as her own.

'The Andaluz and English mercantile families have intermarried for centuries,' Felipe replied when she commented on the fact. My maternal grandmother's maiden name was Sandeman. The characteristics of both nationalities are in my own genes, so the chances of our son having a fair complexion are doubled.'

'You wouldn't mind?' she ventured.

He shrugged. 'Had I minded, I'd hardly have contemplated an English mother for my son and heir.'

'But neither Raine nor I are what you might call well-connected.'

'What *you* might call well-connected, perhaps. The factors I consider of importance have little to do with status. A sound mind in a sound body—those were the main criteria. Although,' he added with a certain grimness, 'I may have miscalculated to a certain extent where your stepsister was concerned. What she did in sending you here in her place all unknowingly was almost as bad as my own response to the realisation.' Dark eyes met blue. 'It's to be hoped that our son will inherit more of his mother's character than my own.'

She said carefully, 'There's no certainty it has even happened yet.'

'If not already, then soon.'

'You said you had no desire for a wife,' she reminded him, and saw his lips slant.

'We're all of us entitled to rethink our attitudes. Everything you said to me was true. I was thinking only of myself. A child needs a mother.'

If she had taught him that much it was worth while, she thought. Perhaps between them they could make something of this marriage, after all. At least they could try.

She found herself unexpectedly hungry when the food came, and did full justice to an excellent gazpacho. Tender asparagus tips were followed by a dish of hake cooked in a savoury sauce and served with French beans and salad. A huge bowl of fresh fruit was provided in lieu of dessert, along with cheese and coffee and a free-ranging choice of liqueurs.

Already mellowed by the wine that had accompanied the meal, Jan settled for a small Tia Maria. Her earlier self-consciousness had dissipated a little as the evening progressed. She was even able to disregard the occasional curious glances from surrounding tables. That Felipe was well-known went without saying; it stood to reason that people would wonder who his companion for the evening was. No doubt news of their marriage would prove a source of gossip for days.

'Do you never entertain?' she asked him on impulse as he lit one of the cheroots he smoked only after dinner.

'Not often,' he acknowledged. He eyed her with a speculative expression. 'You would like to entertain?'

'Not really.' Her smile was diffident. 'I imagine the social round in these parts is pretty daunting.'

'That would depend,' he said, 'on the invitations both given and accepted. There are many who would welcome a return to the days when the Hacienda de Rimados was active in that manner. Since my father's death the occasions have been few and far between. There are only two people I count as true close friends.'

About to say something else, he suddenly altered his expression as his gaze went beyond her, rising to his feet. Jan became aware of someone pausing at the table.

'Felipe!' greeted a warm, seductive voice. 'It is unusual to see you here.'

'Habits were made to be broken,' he rejoined equably. He switched to English to add, 'Janita, I'd like you to meet Sabatine Valverde.'

No more than a year or two older than Jan herself, the newcomer was one of the most beautiful women she had ever seen. Her black hair was parted in the centre and drawn back in a style that only the most perfect features could take, her eyes wide-spaced and the colour of topaz. The look they turned on Jan was oddly intense.

'You are here on holiday, *señorita*?' she asked.

'No.' Jan glanced pleadingly in Felipe's direction, not at all sure what she was supposed to say or do next.

Face composed, voice equally so, he said, 'Janita is my *novia*.'

If he had announced his imminent death he couldn't have created more of an impact. Sabatine's eyes flashed with some inner fire, her body stiffening. 'You are to be married?'

He lifted a well-schooled eyebrow. 'That is the usual progression, I believe. Will you wish us well?'

With a visible effort, she turned her gaze once more in Jan's direction, her smile rigid. 'You must forgive my surprise. No one was aware of any betrothal. When is the wedding to be?'

Felipe answered for her. 'Soon. A small and private affair.'

The man at Sabatine's back, whom she had made no attempt to introduce, stirred uncomfortably. 'We should go to our table,' he murmured.

For a moment she seemed not to hear him. Her attention was for Felipe and Felipe alone. When she spoke it was in Spanish, and too softly for Jan to catch the gist. Then she was moving away, with just the barest nod by way of farewell.

Silence reigned for several moments after the departure. Jan was the first to break it, striving for a casual note. 'She seemed a little put out.'

The reply came smoothly enough. 'She has no cause to be.' Felipe shook his head as she made to speak again. 'The flamenco is about to begin. We'll talk later.'

She turned her face obediently towards the open floor, trying to show an intelligent interest as the black-costumed male dancer began the ritual heel tapping. That Sabatine Valverde was more than just a casual acquaintance was only too obvious. Her reaction to the news had been that of someone knocked for six. What was Felipe to her? More importantly, what was she to Felipe? No cause to be put out, he had said. That statement alone gave rise to speculation.

The man on the floor was joined by a woman wearing an elaborately flounced dress of scarlet and black, their movements, formal and structured at first, building gradually along with the music to a pace and pattern that stirred the blood. Jan joined in the applause when it was over, summoning a smile for Felipe's benefit.

'That was wonderful!'

'Good, but not the best,' he returned. 'Camilla won't appear before midnight. Do you wish to stay?'

She shook her head. 'I doubt if I'm well-versed enough to appreciate the subtleties.'

'You'll learn in time,' he said. 'The true flamenco is sung *cante jondo*—from the depths of the soul. It will all be strange to you for a while, but the English are adaptable, are they not?' He didn't wait for any answer, his voice briskening again. 'We'll leave now before the next performance begins.'

They began the drive back to the *hacienda* in a silence Jan would have liked to regard as companionable, but couldn't. She wanted to know about Sabatine Valverde, yet hesitated to ask. Whatever the relationship between the two of them, it could have little bearing on the present situation, she told herself. Forget the woman. She had enough to occupy her mind without worrying about Felipe's past.

'What do I wear to the wedding?' she asked at length in sheer desperation. 'I don't have anything even remotely suitable.'

'You'll find something in Jerez,' he replied, drawing her a swift glance.

'On my own?'

'I telephoned the Fuentes. They'll be here with us tomorrow evening. Leda will accompany you on your shopping expedition.'

'They must have been surprised,' she murmured.

'But pleased that I take myself a bride at last. Those who find happiness in marriage themselves constantly seek it for others.' He took his eyes from the road for a brief moment to look at her, his smile faint but reassuring. 'You'll like Leda. There are only a few years between you. Like myself, they're both of them without family of their own.'

'What about your cousins?' she asked. 'Don't they count?'

'I was speaking of immediate family,' came the dispassionate response.

'But they will be invited to the wedding?'

His jawline compressed. 'We have little to do with each other.'

The tone of his voice discouraged any further questions. Jan took the hint. Family feuds were outside her province. The less people there, the better, as far as she was concerned. Meeting these friends of Felipe's was going to be quite enough of a strain.

It was well after midnight when they reached the *casa*. The servants were not in evidence, though lights had been left burning.

Felipe paused when they reached the head of the staircase, his expression unrevealing. 'We must part here,' he said. 'Goodnight, Janita.'

It would be unseemly on her part, Jan thought wryly, to question that decision again, although her every sense yearned for some physical contact. He wasn't even going to kiss her, she realised.

'Goodnight,' she said.

He went without a backward glance, leaving her to make her way slowly to her own lonely room. Not for long, she reminded herself. Three nights from now they would share the same bed again as man and wife. If she could only convince herself that she wasn't living through some kind of fantasy!

Leda and Gaspar Fuente spoke English almost as well as Felipe did himself, much to Jan's relief. Although improving, her Spanish was still not up to lengthy conversations. What Felipe had told his friends by way of explanation, she had no way of knowing, but, whatever the Fuentes' thoughts on the subject, they were keeping them strictly under wraps.

Laughing-eyed and attractive, Leda treated Felipe with an easy familiarity which Jan envied. Gaspar was the quieter of the two. About Felipe's age, he grew olives further north, exporting the produce all over the world. Also like Felipe, he could afford to leave his business in the hands of people he trusted.

Shopping with Leda was relatively painless. Jan chose a mid-calf-length dress with a fitted bodice and softly flowing skirt in creamy silk, teaming it with a floppy-brimmed hat and slender-heeled sandals in a slightly darker shade.

It was only when paying for them that she recalled the money Raine had given her. Felipe was due to be returned the whole sum now, of course, but she only had half of it. To offer him that meant admitting to her stepsister's dishonesty, yet there was no way she could raise a further five thousand pounds.

'You look concerned,' commented Leda over the coffee she had suggested before they returned to the *hacienda*. 'Is there something we've forgotten?'

Jan forced a smile, shaking her head. 'Just something I have to sort out with Felipe.' Meeting the friendly gaze across the table, she hesitated only briefly before adding, 'Exactly what has he told you, Leda?'

The shrug was almost apologetic. 'We already knew of his intention. I tried myself to dissuade him from such a course, but he wouldn't listen. It was fortunate that you took the place of your stepsister, although the shock for you must have been great when you realised what it was that Felipe wanted from you.'

'You could say that,' agreed Jan with feeling.

'It was a shock for Gaspar and myself, too, when he telephoned to tell us he was to be married so soon,' Leda added frankly, 'but we're both of us thankful that you found each other.'

Not the whole truth, by any means, Jan acknowledged. Yet better this way than for the Fuentes to know the whole story.

'I suppose it did happen quickly,' she said.

Leda smiled. 'For some, one glance can be enough. I knew the moment I saw Gaspar that he was the only man for me.'

'You don't have any children yourselves yet?'

A cloud passed across the other woman's eyes. 'It has still to happen for us. We're told there is no reason why it should not.'

Jan instinctively tried to reassure her. 'I'm sure it will.'

'That is what we must keep telling ourselves.' Leda made an obvious effort to lighten the moment. 'Yours and Felipe's will perhaps be the first announcement.'

Many a true word, thought Jan wryly. The thought that she might already have life stirring inside her brought an odd sensation. A bare week ago she hadn't even met Felipe. Had it not been for Raine, she never would have met him—might never have known what it was like to lose herself in lovemaking. She ached for his touch, for the feel of his arms about her again. By this time tomorrow she would be his wife. Doña Janita de Rimados. It didn't sound like her at all.

'I suppose you know you're to be the only invited guests at the wedding?' she said. 'I gather there's some estrangement where the family is concerned.'

'There is little love lost,' Leda confirmed. 'The Lobons will be less than happy to hear of Felipe's marriage. The chances of their now inheriting the estates are remote.'

Jan kept her tone purposely light. 'It surprises me that Felipe left it so comparatively late to start thinking about securing the Rimados name when he feels so strongly about it. He can hardly have been deprived of choice.'

Leda laughed. 'It's true to say there are many who would willingly have accepted his proposal had he cared to offer it.'

'Including Sabatine Valverde?'

There was momentary surprise in the eyes opposite. 'You have met Sabatine?'

'Two evenings ago.' Jan paused. 'She's very beautiful.'

'And aware of it.' Her pause was brief. 'Had Felipe wanted it, they would be man and wife already.'

Which meant there had been something between the two of them at some time, Jan concluded. But she had guessed that, hadn't she?

'You have nothing to fear from Sabatine Valverde,' Leda assured her softly, watching her expression. '*You* are the one Felipe chose as his bride.'

Jan summoned a smile, a suitable reply. She and Felipe were the only ones who knew the truth of the matter, and that was how it had to stay. Let Leda keep her illusions.

CHAPTER SIX

LUNCHEON was eaten out on the central patio, with the tinkling of the fountain as a musical accompaniment. Felipe looked relaxed and expansive. He and Gaspar had been out riding most of the morning, it appeared.

'Are you a horsewoman yourself?' Leda asked Jan casually.

'Not really,' she admitted, avoiding so much as a glance in Felipe's direction. 'I tend to fall off.'

'We must see that you have more practise,' he observed on an equable note. 'You'll be safe enough on Santina, providing you don't try to go too fast too soon.'

This time she did look at him, registering the hint of humour in his eyes with a sudden lifting of her spirits. 'I'll try to remember,' she said.

It was a long and lazy afternoon, but not a dull one. Sitting there listening to the conversation flowing around her, and occasionally putting in her own contribution, Jan felt for the first time some measure of confidence. Tomorrow night she would sleep with Felipe as his wife. That fact alone gave her confidence. He might not love her the way she would have preferred the man she married to do, but he both wanted and needed her, and that was a good enough substitute for the present. She almost hoped she was already carrying his child, because that would cleave them even closer.

She followed him when he went to the study at four, determined to sort out the matter of the money he had handed over to Raine.

'I can't offer the whole sum back,' she said after explaining her mission, 'but I haven't touched the five thousand Raine gave to me.'

Felipe had listened without reaction up to that point. When he spoke, it was on a curt note. 'The money is tainted. I want no part of it.'

She looked at him helplessly. 'But what am I supposed to do with it?'

'Whatever you like. Send it back to your sister, if you prefer.' His lip curled a little. 'She appears to have few scruples.'

Jan could hardly argue with that finding. Not that she had any intention of furthering Raine's moral decline by doing as he suggested.

'It isn't mine,' she insisted. 'I want no part of it, either.'

'But you have it,' he responded hardily. 'In your name, in your bank. That's an end to it. The matter is closed.'

There was no doubting that he meant every word. Any further pursuit would only serve to anger him, and that was the last thing she wanted on this the eve of their wedding.

'Is it considered unlucky in Spain for the bride and groom to spend their last evening in each other's company?' she asked with deliberate lightness, and saw his mouth widen into a reluctant smile.

'If it is, I don't subscribe to such superstition. This evening we all of us spend together. Tomorrow, after the wedding, Leda and Gaspar must return to their home. By then, you and I will be in Sevilla.'

'Seville?' Jan was genuinely puzzled. 'You have business there?'

He slanted a lip. 'Are you not entitled to a honeymoon?'

'I hadn't even thought about it,' she confessed. She added haltingly, 'You don't have to subscribe to tradition, either. I'd be quite happy to stay here.'

'We go to Sevilla,' he stated. 'The fashion houses there are superior to any you'll find in Jerez.'

'Oh, I see.' She was suddenly deflated again. 'I'm to outfit myself as befits the wife of a Rimados?'

Felipe looked surprised. 'Is the purchase of a new wardrobe not the dearest wish of every woman?'

Not this one, she thought wryly. She forced a smile, a light shrug. 'One of them, perhaps. I could do with taking Leda along.'

'*I* shall accompany you,' he said. 'Otherwise, I have a feeling you'll spend only the barest minimum. If we're to entertain on our return, you'll need suitable gowns.'

Jan's head snapped up. 'I thought you weren't interested in the social scene?'

It was his turn to shrug. 'The speed and apparent secrecy of our marriage will be the subject of much speculation. Keeping you to myself would only add fuel to the fire.'

'There's still time to call it off,' she responded softly, not all that certain what she wanted his answer to be.

An indecipherable expression came and went in his eyes. 'Too late,' he declared flatly. 'The marriage takes place as arranged. Go now, and leave me to work.'

Jan left him, aware of mixed emotions. There was to be no last-minute reprieve.

Despite the absence of a formal guest-list, the little white church was crowded to the doors. Standing at the altar while the priest conducted the ceremony, Jan felt detached—as if this was happening to someone else, not herself.

It took the firm pressure of Felipe's hand under her arm as they emerged at last into sunlight again to bring the full import home. She was a Rimados now. For the rest of her life this country of his would be hers, too—their children Spanish by law. Had Felipe loved her, none of that would have mattered. Only he didn't believe in love. Not her kind, anyway. She had to learn to live with that knowledge.

The villagers had set up trestle-tables around the central square. Flanked by Leda and Gaspar, bride and groom were allotted place of honour. Food and wine were in abundance. Jan ate too little of the former and drank too much of the latter, desperate to release herself from the strait-jacket constricting her every move. She was suddenly glad they were going to Seville; glad to have some time to become accustomed to her new position. One day she would look back on this uncertainty and laugh. One day.

The villagers were still celebrating when they left them in the late afternoon. Leda and Gaspar made their farewells at the house, the former giving Jan a sisterly hug before getting into the waiting car.

'You must come and visit with us as soon as it can be arranged,' she said. 'Take care of her, Felipe.'

'I intend to,' he answered meaningfully.

With all the household staff enjoying the wedding festivities, the house was still and silent. Laid out in the room they were to share on their return were the things in which they were to travel. Jan stiffened a little despite herself as Felipe came up behind her to unfasten the tiny buttons at the back of her dress, feeling his breath warm on the nape of her neck, the light, caressing touch of his lips on her skin.

'You're beautiful,' he murmured. 'More than I deserve.'

'How long will it take us to reach Seville?' she asked huskily, and sensed his withdrawal even before he moved back away from her.

'Two hours. We'll be in good time for dinner.'

And afterwards they would retire together to the marital bed. She trembled at the thought. Perhaps in Felipe's arms she could finally convince herself that today was no dream.

She wore a simple suit in blue linen for the journey. Felipe himself was comfortable and casual in cream trousers and shirt. Their suitcases were already stowed in the silver-grey Mercedes that waited outside. Jan glanced back as they turned out through the gates, seeing the imposing bulk of the house from a new perspective. Her home now and for always. But would she ever know true happiness there?

They drove towards Jerez in order to take the Cádiz-Seville motorway, making fast time on a road almost empty of traffic. The approach to Seville itself Jan found both bleak and ugly, with factories and cheap housing developments to either hand for several miles. Then suddenly the road broadened, with parks and squares and graciously soaring buildings to one side, while to the other lay the Guadalquivir river arced by bridges of smoke-grey stone.

Their hotel was in the older part of the city, a small but opulently furnished place where uniformed staff greeted Felipe with the deference Jan herself was beginning to accept as his due. Their suite was panelled throughout in mahogany, the bed a huge brass affair, plump with pillows and covered in the finest lacework. The great enamelled bowl of a bath would comfortably hold three people, Jan considered, bemused by so much munificence.

She found the view from the balcony more African than European, with minarets and arches and rustling date-palm. Sunset lent a golden glow to the white stone, outlining the soaring tower of the Giralda against a sky already turning from blue to violet as night stole over the city.

'You would like to go out to dinner?' asked Felipe when she turned back into the room at last. 'Or perhaps to stay here?'

'Here,' she said after a moment. 'If that's all right with you?'

'So polite,' he mocked lightly. 'I am yours to command, *mi pequêra*.'

That, she thought as he moved to lift the telephone receiver, would be the day!

Dinner was brought to the suite, served by two impeccably mannered young waiters. Jan found herself surprisingly hungry, but she avoided the wine. The very thought of what was to come was stimulus enough. Her whole body trembled at the memory of what it was like to lie in Felipe's arms. Man and wife; it still didn't seem real.

At her suggestion, they sat out for a while on the balcony, drinking in the sights and sounds of night-time Seville. The air was soft and balmy on the skin, the faint breeze just stirring Jan's hair. Tomorrow Felipe was to take her around the sights of the city. After that he was to introduce her to the fashion houses from which she would henceforth obtain her clothes. The latter experience was one she viewed with trepidation. No more popping into M&S or Next. From now on, she would dress to suit her new role in life.

Restless, she rose to view the scene from a different angle, standing with hands resting lightly on the balustrade as she looked out over the illuminated city.

'It's so beautiful!' she said softly. 'I can't believe I'm really here.'

'We're both here.' Felipe was standing right behind her, his movements so quiet that she hadn't been aware of his leaving the chair. His hands came about her waist, sliding up to cup both breasts, thumbs gently brushing her nipples. 'The past three days have seemed a lifetime,' he murmured against her ear. 'I've missed you, Janita.'

Not wholly what she wanted to hear, she thought mistily, but close enough for the present. She leaned her weight back against him, thrilling to his lean strength. Her husband—the man with whom she would spend each and every night of her life from this moment on. His very touch set her on fire.

He turned her towards him, eyes lit by an inner glow in the dark tautness of his face. His mouth was passionate, drawing her heart and soul into her answering embrace. Without speaking again, he took her by the hand and led her back into the room.

On both other occasions when she had been with him she had already been stripped of her clothing. This time he did the undressing for her, slowly and with a sensuality that had her quivering with expectancy.

Laying her on the bed, he began by just stroking her with his fingertips, starting at her ankle and working his way along the length of her until her whole body tingled. She was mindless with desire, offering herself to him with an abandonment she would never have imagined herself capable of such a short time ago. His lips teased brief kisses over her breasts, her stomach and down over the quivering flesh of her belly to reach the very centre

of her being, making her gasp and writhe in an ecstasy
of sensation she wanted never to stop.

When at last he came over her she was past all rational
thought. All she wanted was his weight, his heat, his
mind-shattering possession—hers for all time.

Those first few days went by like a dream. As a husband,
Felipe was everything any woman could want, Jan often
thought. If the actual words of love were lacking, that
was certainly all that *was* lacking. In every other way he
fulfilled her deepest desires.

Visiting the fashion houses turned out to be far from
the ordeal she had somehow imagined. The name of
Rimados had only to be mentioned to conjure immediate and respectful attention. Left to her own devices,
Jan would have scarcely known which of the outfits pa-
raded before her to even try on, but Felipe knew no such
doubt. What it must all be costing, she couldn't begin
to imagine. Prices were never mentioned. Not, at least,
in her hearing.

The bullfights were the only things at which she
balked. Not for anything, she declared, was she going
to watch a dumb animal being systematically tortured
to death in the name of sport. Felipe made no attempt
to pressure her, nor did he appear particularly perturbed
by her views. Instead they spent an afternoon at Casa
Lonja, scrutinising some of the thousands of maps,
manuscripts and other documents describing what the
Spanish explorers had found on discovering the New
World of the Indies and Americas.

But it was the nights she lived for. Making love with
Felipe was an experience of which she thought she could
never tire. He was passionate, demanding, yet with moments of tenderness that created real hope in her heart

for an eventual deepening of emotion between them. Even lacking that ultimate assurance, she was happier than she had ever been.

Their return to the *hacienda* was in no way an anticlimax. From mistress of the man to mistress of the house in one short week wasn't bad going, Jan acknowledged whimsically, relinquishing her brief attempt to persuade Yola to allow her to do her own unpacking.

Hung reverently away, the new garments overflowed into the empty wardrobe. There were outfits for every foreseeable occasion, complete with matching accessories. The only cloud on the immediate horizon was the thought of meeting all the people who inhabited this new world of hers—of facing the inevitable curiosity. One sure question would be how the two of them had met in the first place.

'You were here on holiday,' Felipe improvised when she put the matter to him. 'I almost ran you down with my car, took you to dinner to compensate—the rest, as they say, is history.' His smile was only slightly sardonic. 'I was never the traditionalist in my habits.'

That, Jan could well believe. 'The staff here know the truth,' she pointed out tentatively. 'Supposing someone talks?'

The compression of his jaw told its own story. 'They value their positions here too much to take that risk. Added to which, you earned loyalty when you saved Carlos from my anger.'

'At the cost of my own freedom,' she responded lightly, and saw the familiar mockery spring again in his eyes.

'A spurious freedom at best. You were my property from the moment you put your name to that first contract, to say nothing of the second.

'No one can *own* another person,' Jan objected with a certain asperity. 'That went out with slavery!'

'You belong to me.' The statement was unequivocal. 'As will our children in their turn. Make no mistake about that!'

Arguing that point would obviously be a waste of time and effort, Jan conceded, biting back the quick retort. She had known from the first how far apart in some respects were their ideals. Time and patience would bridge the gap, she comforted herself. She had plenty of the one, and she would cultivate the other. This marriage of theirs had to work out.

Felipe's suggestion a couple of days later that they hold their first social gathering was received with misgivings. Just a small dinner-party to begin with, he said. There would be opportunity after the harvest was in to consider a more elaborate affair.

The 'small' dinner-party turned out to mean invitations being sent to no less than a dozen couples. Jan registered without comment the name of Sabatine Valverde on the list Felipe himself had drawn up, loath to acknowledge any lingering doubts where the Spanish woman was concerned. As Leda had said, had he wanted to marry Sabatine, he would have done so.

All the same, she could hardly fail to be aware of the enmity in the other woman's eyes on meeting her again. The man accompanying her was the same one who had been with her the first time. Named Luis Fernández, he was a little younger than Felipe, yet obviously a man of means. A very suitable match, Jan would have thought.

Her grasp of the Spanish language was put to the test by her left-hand partner at dinner, who, unusually for the area, spoke very little English. Occasionally she caught Felipe's eye from the head of the table, and was reassured by his approving nod. In time she might even find herself able to take these events in her stride, she reflected wryly, although right now the effort was telling on her. She was the only foreigner here tonight, and it showed.

In true Spanish tradition, the meal itself had not been served until ten o'clock. By eleven-thirty Jan could feel herself flagging. It was unlikely that people would even begin to think of leaving before one o'clock. How she was going to keep her eyes open, much less take an intelligent part in conversation, she hesitated to think.

Coffee served through in the *salón* was some help. Jan forced herself to move from group to group of her guests, weathering the occasional sly comment, the speculative question. Slipping out at one point to refresh her make-up in the ground-floor cloakroom, she was somehow unsurprised to find that Sabatine had followed her. Dressed in scarlet, the other woman looked more beautiful than ever, she thought. She summoned a smile she hoped did not reveal her inner feelings.

'It's so warm in there with all those people, don't you find?'

Sabatine ignored the comment. 'Felipe must have been desperate indeed to offer marriage to someone so obviously unsuited to our way of life,' she stated without preamble. 'You will never be the kind of wife a man in his position needs. I hope you realise that.'

It took Jan a moment or two to form a reply. When she did speak, it was with control. 'Could this be sour grapes because he married me instead of you, by any chance?'

The full red mouth took on a contemptuous curl. 'I could have been his wife had I agreed to bear him the son he craves. Felipe would deny himself anything to ensure the continuance of his name—even his own emotional needs.'

Blue eyes held topaz, refusing to flinch away. 'So why didn't you agree?'

'I have no desire for children.'

'Noble of you to be honest about it,' Jan managed, and felt the full impact of the angry glitter.

'Make no mistake,' the older woman stated softly, 'you are only here for a purpose. Once he has what he needs from you, he will soon put you aside.'

'That remains to be seen.' Not for anything, Jan told herself, was she going to reveal her inner feelings. 'If you'll excuse me,' she added politely, 'I have to get back to our other guests.'

'They are all amused by you,' came the spiteful comment. 'So pitifully inadequate, that is what they are saying.'

'Not for long.' Jan was already at the door. 'I learn quickly.'

Outside again, she steadied her breathing. Allowing Sabatine's obvious jealousy to get to her would be stupid. All the same, the words had penetrated. The other would have filled to perfection the position she herself was finding such a struggle. Felipe himself had obviously believed it—no doubt still did. Only the continuance of the Rimados name had to come first, no matter what. It was an obsession with him.

Without meaning to, she found herself watching him during the rest of that interminable evening, registering how often he and Sabatine seemed to gravitate together. On more than one occasion she crossed glances with Luis Fernández, aware of a certain empathy in his wry smile. If he was in love with Sabatine, she felt sorry for him.

Falling in love with someone incapable of returning the emotion was a futile practice.

Sabatine and Felipe were of a kind, she supposed, when it came right down to it. He had to compare the two of them, and to her detriment. All she could give him was a child—and perhaps not even that. What kind of a future could they look forward to if they remained childless?

The last of the guests left around two o'clock. Jan felt sorry for the servants who still had to clear away the debris, although they seemed to accept the late hour as a matter-of-course.

Felipe had little to say as they prepared for bed. He must be thinking about the Spanish woman, Jan surmised with growing certitude. She scarcely knew whether to be glad or sorry when he offered no more than a token kiss before settling down for what was left of the night. From now on she was never going to be sure whether it was her or Sabatine he imagined he held in his arms.

Her mood on waking remained depressed, lightened only a little by Felipe's invitation to accompany him to the winery. It was time, he said, that she began to understand something of the business that made the name of Rimados what it was.

They left at ten, covering the twenty kilometres to Jerez in less than half an hour in the powerful car. Stretching through the town were streets of inaptly named wine cellars, big, high buildings with grilled windows through which the heady scent of sherry permeated the air.

A pair of wrought-iron gates bearing the family crest opened as if by some pre-arranged signal to admit them into a courtyard bright with flowering plants. Inside, the office building was welcomingly cool and dim after the glare of the sun on white stone. Felipe led the way through to a luxuriously furnished reception area, and from there into a room not unlike his study at the *hacienda*.

Even as Jan took a seat on the deep leather sofa, an elderly man appeared bearing a tray loaded with bottles and glasses and small plates of what looked like canapés. These he commenced to set out on a small darkwood sideboard.

'Before I show you around the *bodegas*,' Felipe announced when the man had departed again, 'I'll introduce you to the local custom of drinking sherry.' He was pouring as he spoke, half filling two of the inwardly curving glasses from one of the three ready-opened bottles. 'First the cream, then the amontillado, and finally the fino, which we then stay with for the rest of the day.'

'I'm not sure,' Jan murmured, 'that I can drink three glasses straight off.'

'You don't need to,' he said. 'Just a few sips from each glass is enough to give your palate the taste. At lunch we'll continue to drink the fino with our meal.'

He brought the first glass across to her, along with one of the plates of little tartlets, eyes narrowing a little as they rested on her face. 'You look less than your usual self this morning,' he observed. 'Last night was so tiring?'

'I'm not used to the hours you keep over here yet,' she returned with an attempt at lightness. 'At home we're usually finishing dinner by ten at the latest, not starting it!'

'This is your home now,' he returned without sympathy, 'so you'll have to get used to our ways. Next weekend we're invited to the Murillo estate. Domingo breeds fighting bulls. I trust your feelings for the creatures will be kept to yourself while we're there.'

'I'll do my best.' She was promising nothing. 'I can't help the way I feel.'

Dark eyes took on a certain intolerance. 'You English take this animal idolatry to extremes at times!'

'Caring for the dumb and helpless is no great fault,' she flashed. 'Don't worry, I've no intention of making an issue of it with the Murillos. I doubt if my opinion would count for much with them, anyway.'

Felipe lifted a sardonic lip. 'As my wife, your opinion is of some importance to most. Never doubt that. Are you ready to try the amontillado now?'

Jan had drained the first glass without even realising it, the warm glow in her stomach its own testimonial. 'Why not?' she said recklessly. 'This is one Spanish custom I don't have any quarrel with.'

He moved to take up fresh glasses, pouring from the second bottle for them both. She took half of the contents in one swallow, relishing the difference in both taste and sweetness.

'You must eat something,' Felipe invited, indicating the plate of tartlets he had left on the low table in front of her. 'Otherwise, it will go to your head.'

It was doing that already, she acknowledged. She wished he would sit down. Standing like that, he seemed to tower over her. Her husband, yet a stranger still in almost every sense. What was she doing here in this place—in this country? She didn't belong; she never would belong. There was too much that was alien to her way of thought.

Her third glass, of pale, delicate fino, she treated with more caution, setting it down after the first sip. 'If you're going to show me round the *bodega*, it had better be now, while I can still walk straight,' she said with an attempt at humour. 'It wouldn't do for the boss's wife to fall flat on her face in front of *hoi polloi*!'

'I'll be there to keep you upright,' came the smooth rejoinder. 'As you say, we have a position to uphold.'

With the approach of noon, the heat outside was a tangible weight. It was a relief to step through the huge door of the nearest cellar into the vast, vaulted dimness. Rows of butts spread out and upwards, with walkways in between.

There were no vintage years in sherry, Jan learned over the following hour. The idea was to achieve a uniform wine, recognisable by its quality and taste as much as by name. Casks were stacked in tiers, the bottom one of which contained wine ready for sale. The quantity drawn off was then made up by refilling from the next cask up, which held wine a year younger, and so on up the scales until the fifth year and youngest wine was reached.

There was more detail, much of which she failed take in. Her head was buzzing from the wine she had drunk earlier, her mood depressive. What use was the knowledge going to be to her, anyway? she wondered. This was probably the only time she would ever visit Felipe's place of work.

As if registering her lack of concentration, he cut the tour short after the second *bodega*. The whole thing had been a simple token gesture on his part, Jan thought. He neither expected nor needed her appreciation of the family business. Her role was already set out for her—to produce the son who would one day take over all this. Always providing that the son would want the same things his father wanted, of course. With her blood in his veins, he might well have different ideas. That was something else to consider, far in the future though that time may be.

They were back at the *hacienda* by one-thirty. Luncheon was served outside at two o'clock. Jan forced herself to eat something from every dish served to her, and sip sparingly of the fino Felipe insisted on pouring for them both. Viewing the lean features across the table as she replaced her glass, she felt oddly detached. Enough so to feel no surprise at the question that came involuntarily to her lips.

'Is it true you asked Sabatine Valverde to marry you?'

For a fleeting moment the dark head seemed to freeze. When he lifted his gaze towards her, however, there was no hint of discomfiture in his expression. 'Yes,' he acknowledged.

She swallowed thickly, already regretful of having brought the subject up. 'Was a son more important to you than your feelings for her?' she asked, and saw a shadow pass across his eyes.

'My feelings have no bearing,' he stated flatly. 'I thought you understood that.'

'In relationship to myself, perhaps.' Her head was up, her gaze equally devoid of expression. 'Although guilt itself is an emotion of sorts, I suppose. Sabatine would have made you a much more suitable wife than I ever will.'

His shrug was a stab in the heart. 'You're probably right. She's well versed in all the social graces you still have to acquire.'

'She's also a very beautiful woman.'

His smile was mirthless. 'I'd noticed. As you can only have gained this knowledge through Sabatine herself, I assume she also told you her reasons for refusing me?'

'If you made the offer conditional, I'm not surprised she refused. Most women would.' She caught the irony in his glance, flushing a little. '*I* wasn't given the choice, was I?'

'No,' he admitted, still without visible reaction. 'Neither, in the end, did I leave myself with any choice. Poetic justice, wouldn't you say?'

'There's nothing poetic in a loveless marriage,' Jan responded bitterly. 'We're two people caught in the same trap, that's all.'

His brows lifted, the mockery hard-edged. 'But with compensations.'

'Except that I haven't come up with yours yet.' With deliberation, she added, 'And perhaps never shall.'

'If not, it won't be for want of effort,' he promised grimly. 'It's too late for regrets.'

On either side, Jan acknowledged. They had to make the best of what they had together.

If only she could convince herself that Sabatine Valverde no longer held any place in his scheme of things to come.

CHAPTER SEVEN

SITUATED out on the coastal plains towards Tarifa, the Murillo ranch was a two-hour drive. Once off the main road, they were soon running between fenced pastures, with the occasional lone bull in evidence sheltering from the sun in the shadow of a tree. Massive, and carrying sweeping horns, they nevertheless looked so quiet and calm, it was difficult to equate them with the power-packed death-machines of the *corrida*.

'Seed bulls,' Felipe explained when Jan said as much. 'The bravest and most aggressive kept for breeding purposes. Don't be deceived by appearances. They'll seldom charge in the heat of the day unless provoked, but they're still dangerous. More so, perhaps, than any other creature on earth. A *toro bravo* has even been known to dispatch an elephant.' He added, 'Domingo will be holding a trial at his corral this weekend to test his young stock. It offers an opportunity for those who harbour a desire to take part in a *corrida*.'

Jan glanced at him swiftly. 'Are you speaking from experience?'

'I've been in the ring,' he acknowledged.

'Why take such a risk?'

He considered the question, eyes on the narrow road ahead. 'The challenge,' he said at length. 'To pit one's wits against an animal so fast and powerful and emerge unscathed brings satisfaction of a kind few can appreciate.'

'You'll be taking part this weekend, too?'

'Perhaps.' He glanced her way, mouth sardonic. 'You'd object?'

This time she kept her own gaze averted. 'I don't have any jurisdiction over your actions.'

'Nor enough concern to try, apparently.' His tone had shortened. 'Should I be killed, you'd be rid of any obligation, yes?'

'That wasn't on my mind!' she denied with asperity. 'I don't want you dead.'

'Perhaps emasculated, then? That way you'd no longer need to fight your baser inclinations.'

She said thickly, 'I'm not sure what that's supposed to mean.'

'Do you imagine me so dense that I fail to recognise the difference between involuntary and whole-hearted participation?' came the scathing comment. 'Your body has a will of its own, *querida*. One your newly acquired reluctance fails to overcome. The fact that I once asked another woman to be my wife has no bearing on our relationship.'

'It underlines just how ruthless you really are,' she responded on a harder note. 'Any child we have will be mine as well as yours. I hope you'll remember that.'

The strong mouth twisted. 'I doubt if I'll be allowed to forget it.'

'Always providing it actually happens, of course.' Her tone held deliberation. 'So far, there's no sign.'

'Then I must redouble my efforts,' he returned coolly.

Jan bit her lip, hating herself all the more for the leap her pulses had given. All she was to him was a breeding animal. This marriage was to be permanent and binding, he had decreed, but she doubted if that vow would survive a failure on her part to conceive. The question was, how long would he give her before calling it a day?

The ranch-house was traditionally Spanish, set around
a central courtyard. Opening on to the covered balcony
which skirted the whole building at first-floor level, the
room they were to occupy for the coming two nights had
its own adjoining bathroom. Felipe elected to take a
shower while Jan sorted out her things, and he emerged
with towel wrapped about his lean hips to seek fresh
clothing.

'Put on something casual for the moment,' he advised
when she asked the tentative question. 'There'll be plenty
of time to change again before dinner.'

'There seemed a lot of people already here,' she commented, trying to maintain indifference as he dropped
the towel to pull on a pair of briefs. 'Were we the last
arrivals, do you think?'

'I doubt it.' His tone was perfectly level. 'Sabatine is
yet to come, to mention but one. Carlotta and she are
cousins. Had you not seen the family resemblance?'

'It hadn't occurred to me to look for it.' She paused
before adding, 'Will she be bringing Luis with her?'

'Perhaps.' He sounded suddenly shorter. 'He appears
to be her regular escort these days.'

A fact he didn't care for, Jan surmised, reading between the lines. And what of Sabatine herself? Was she
contemplating eventual marriage with the other man, or
was he simply a means of arousing Felipe's jealousy?
The latter had wanted a son badly enough to put other
considerations aside, but that didn't mean he'd stopped
feeling. Few men could fail to be stirred by a woman as
beautiful as Sabatine.

She put on a simply cut though madly expensive
trouser suit in her favourite off-white to go down in,
relieved to see that the other women were also casually
dressed. Over the following half-hour or so she met many

people, although retaining few names. Several compli-
mented her on her Spanish, much to her pleasure. She
was beginning to get a real feel for the language at last.

Sabatine put in an appearance as day was beginning
to drift towards night, Luis in tow. From where she sat,
momentarily alone, on the edge of the central fountain,
Jan saw her greet Felipe, looking into his eyes as if no
one else existed for her. Luis left them to it, to meander
a course that brought him eventually into Jan's vicinity.

'It is good to see you again,' he said easily. 'You would
like your glass refilling, perhaps?'

Jan shook her head. 'Thank you, I've had enough for
the present.' She smiled at the man, who was making
no attempt to move on. 'Shall you be taking part in this
trial tomorrow, Luis?'

His shrug was light. 'Only the brave among us do that.'

'Or the foolhardy.'

'I think,' he observed, 'that you disapprove of our
national sport?'

'In a word, yes,' she said. 'But then there are so-called
English sports involving animals that I disapprove of,
too.' She looked for a change of subject, too well aware
that her opinion could be construed as inflammatory.
'Have you known Sabatine long?' was what she came
up with, not altogether intentionally.

'Several weeks,' he acknowledged. His gaze went back
to where his partner still stood at Felipe's side—although
they had now been joined by others—taking on that same
wryness Jan had noted on the night of the dinner-party.
'She and your husband are old friends, it appears.'

'Yes.' She could trust herself to go no further. She
added brightly, 'It's almost eight. Time I thought about
changing for dinner. I'm not really used to the hours

you people keep yet. Back home we're thinking about bed when you're only just sitting down to your meal!'

'You still think of England as your home?' asked Luis on a curious note. 'Should not a wife accept her husband's domicile as her own?'

Jan lifted her shoulders in a brief shrug. 'It takes time.' Smile fixed, she came to her feet. 'Excuse me, will you, Luis?'

She wasn't alone in leaving the assembly. Several other of the women had already retired, presumably for the same purpose. The dress Jan had selected to wear for dinner was a melting blue in colour, with a tightly fitting bodice and narrow shoulder-straps. Slender-heeled sandals and an evening-bag were an exact match.

Opening the flat jeweller's case, she gazed for a lengthy moment at the diamond and sapphire necklace and bracelet Felipe had bought her as a wedding present, still feeling they were only hers on loan. Materially, this marriage of hers provided everything any woman could possibly dream about, yet it couldn't make up for what was missing. Nothing could.

She was attempting to fasten the necklace's clasp when Felipe entered the room. He came to do the job for her, his face, reflected in the mirror, revealing little of what he was thinking.

'You seem tense,' he remarked, allowing the necklace to fall into position about her throat. 'You need have no concern regarding my intentions for the moment, I assure you.'

'It hadn't occurred to me that I might,' she denied, unable to keep her tone as calm and cool as she would have liked. 'After all, you're hardly going to tear off a dress you spent so much money on!'

His expression darkened. 'The cost is of no concern to me.'

'The look of it, then. I only brought one for each evening, and I can hardly wear the same thing twice in present company, can I?'

Hands like twin vices clamped down hard on her shoulders, cutting into the bone. 'If you wish to arouse my anger,' he said grimly, 'you're well on the way to succeeding! What is it you want from me?'

'Nothing you can give me,' she flashed. 'Unless it's to let me go.'

Something flickered in the dark eyes at her back. 'We have a contract to fulfil,' he stated flatly. He released her, turning away with an abruptness more hurtful than his fingers had been. 'Wait for me.'

Jan stood where she was without moving until the bathroom door had closed behind him, only then easing rigid muscles. There had been moments during their time in Seville when she had been convinced that something worth while could grow from what they had shared, but it had proved a worthless dream. They could never be close in any way that really counted.

Dinner was a seven-course feast. Seated between Luis and another man named Carlos something or other, Jan allowed conversation to form an excuse for only picking at each plate. Felipe had a seat next to Sabatine—whether by accident or design, there was no way of telling. She couldn't allow herself to care, she thought resolutely. If she were stuck with this marriage, and all it entailed, then she had little recourse but to make the best of it as it stood. Once she became pregnant, Felipe might leave her alone.

A thought that brought little comfort.

If Luis entertained similar suspicions over the table placings, he was keeping them well-concealed. He was from Madrid, Jan learned. Apparently of private means, he had come originally to Jerez to stay with relatives.

'My mother's cousin was hoping for a greater alliance between our two families by marrying me to his daughter,' he acknowledged frankly. 'Had I not met Sabatine, I may well have allowed myself to be swayed into a betrothal. Elena was eager enough.'

'I gather you're not staying with them any longer?' Jan surmised.

His mouth slanted. 'It seemed prudent to leave. After meeting Sabatine, I could no longer contemplate even the possibility of marriage with any other woman.'

Heart jerking, she said softly, 'Are you going to marry her?'

'I have asked her, but she gives me no answer as yet.' He sounded suddenly despondent. 'I cannot put off my return to Madrid for very much longer.'

'Perhaps,' Jan suggested with care, 'she simply doesn't want to leave Jerez. Could you live here yourself?'

He shook his smooth dark head. 'Madrid is where I belong—where the name Fernàndez has importance. In Jerez I am nothing, because I have no part in the wine business. Had Sabatine not invited me here this weekend, I would not have been accorded the honour.'

A social closed shop, Jan reflected. That about summed it up. She was a part of this gathering only on sufferance herself. It gave her a sense of affinity with the man at her side.

'You'll work it out,' she soothed. 'One way or another.'

There was a modicum of self-interest in that hope, she acknowledged wryly as Luis's attention was momentarily claimed by his other partner. If he managed to persuade Sabatine to go with him to Madrid, that would be at least one source of concern removed from her life. The operative word being 'if', of course.

Midnight came and went without apparent note by anyone but Jan herself. Her eyelids felt heavy, her brain numbed by the endless flow of conversation about the long table. A general move to the *salón* around one o'clock brought some slight relief, but it didn't last. It was in sheer desperation that she finally had to slip outside for some fresh air.

No one would miss her for a few minutes, she reassured herself, leaning thankfully against warm stone as she listened to the soothing sound of the fountain. Even if they did, it wasn't all that important. It was good to be alone again, cut off from those inside by the glass doors at her back. She would never in a million years become a part of this scene. She didn't really want to be a part of it. These people were alien to her.

Behind her, the door opened again to emit a male figure, the sounds from within surging and fading as it was closed once more.

'I saw you come out here,' said Luis. 'It seemed an excellent idea. Of course, we must risk the mosquitoes.'

'There don't seem to be any around.' She was trying not to resent the intrusion. 'In any case, it has to be worth a few bites just to be alone for a while.' She flushed in the semi-darkness as he shot her a glance. 'I'm sorry, I didn't mean to imply what that sounded like. It's just that I felt stifled in there.'

'No more than I did myself.' The darkly handsome face had relaxed again. 'We are both of us on the outside in more ways than just the one.' One hand lifted to pat an inside pocket of his white dinner-jacket. 'You would object if I light a cheroot?'

'Not at all.' Jan kept her voice light. 'It will help keep any flying stock at bay.'

There was silence for a moment while he busied himself with case and lighter. Only after he had lit up, and had taken the first deep pull on the slim brown tube, did he say softly, 'How did you come to marry a man so cold as Felipe, Janita?'

Her laugh was forced. 'Isn't that a rather presumptuous question on such short acquaintance?'

'Perhaps.' He was unabashed. 'But I would still like to know the answer. You have no love for him, I think.'

The muscles around her heart contracted. 'He's what back home we call a "good catch",' she responded with deliberation. 'Isn't that reason enough?'

'For many,' he agreed. 'For you, I would have imagined love of some importance, too.'

'You don't know me,' she rejoined. 'How can you possibly guess what might be of importance to me?'

His sigh came deep. 'You are right, of course. There is no certainty in instinct. I *know* Sabatine to be the only woman for me, but her own emotions are not yet clear to me. I could only wish that they were.'

Jan said with control, 'She hasn't actually refused you yet. All you can do is keep hoping. You have a lot to offer, Luis.'

'But not, I fear, enough.'

Jan doubted it, too. Compared with Felipe, Luis was small fry. Given time and opportunity, Sabatine might well have changed her mind about supplying the former with the child he wanted. It would have been a small enough return for all she would have stood to gain. Her refusal had been too quick, too unstudied—perhaps because she had believed him incapable of holding out against his desire for her; she was just about arrogant enough for that. Whatever, she was by no means ready to give up all hope of reclaiming what she had lost. That was only too evident.

'I think I'd better go back in,' she said. 'Is it likely to go on for very much longer, do you think?'

Luis lifted his shoulders. 'The night is still young. Perhaps another hour before people begin to retire.'

Her smile was wry. 'I'm not sure I can last out! Nice talking with you, anyway, Luis. I only wish I could offer you some comfort.'

'Having someone listen to my problems has been a comfort,' he responded. 'There is no one here in whom I can confide.'

She would as soon not have been the recipient of his hopes and dreams, Jan reflected. Especially not when they concerned Sabatine Valverde. The woman was using him, that was all.

He stayed to finish the cheroot while she went back inside. Felipe was directly facing her across the *salón* when she slipped through the door, with Sabatine for once absent from the group of which he was a member. Apart from a faint lift of one eyebrow, he showed no reaction. But then, why should he? She had done nothing wrong in leaving the company for a few minutes.

Someone else claimed her attention. Fighting off weariness, Jan allowed herself to be drawn into conversation. Tomorrow, she promised herself, she would put the siesta period to good purpose and catch up on her sleep. That way she might manage to get through the next evening. She would be heartily thankful when the weekend was over. It was proving a strain in more ways than the one.

Felipe's appearance at her elbow came as a surprise, because she had thought him still embroiled in discussion across the room. He looked wonderful in a dinner-jacket, she thought fleetingly, his breadth of shoulder enhanced by the superb cut and fit of the creamy white material. Meeting his eyes, she felt a sudden inner recoil from the steely impenetrability. A cold man, Luis had called him. Right at this moment the description fitted like a glove.

'I think it time we retired,' he said. 'Come and take your leave of our hostess.'

From Carlotta's lack of protest at their going, it seemed likely that she herself was about ready to call it a day. As they went from the room, others were beginning to make the appropriate noises. Felipe made no attempt to touch her as they mounted the wide staircase, yet she could sense the tension in him—like a coiled spring waiting to be released. Wound up by Sabatine, she thought cynically. Well, he needn't imagine he was going to use her as surrogate this time!

The curtains had been drawn in their room, the bed already turned down. Only one lamp was burning, creating an atmosphere of intimacy, despite the size of the room.

'I'll get ready first tonight, if you don't mind,' said Jan diffidently. 'I'm really tired.'

Felipe turned slowly to face her, tossing the dinner-jacket he had just taken off on to a nearby chair. The black cummerbund emphasised the narrowness of his waist, his leanness of hip, creating havoc with her equilibrium. She wanted him so much it was a pain inside her.

'Before we go any further,' he clipped, 'you'll tell me exactly how long you were outside tonight with Luis Fernández.'

She gazed at him, too taken aback by the force of the question to answer for a moment. When she did finally find her voice, it was on a note of defiance she hadn't really intended. 'If you were watching us, you must already know how long.'

'I saw you come in,' he said, 'and a few moments afterwards, Luis following you.' His eyes were narrowed, mouth like a steel trap. 'I was by no means alone in noting the fact.'

'Probably not in reading too much into it, either,' she flashed. 'We talked, that's all.'

'You could have done that without going outside together.'

'We didn't,' she denied. 'Go out together, I mean. I was out there before Luis came.'

'You're telling me it was purely coincidental that he should choose to take some air at that time?'

'No, not quite. He knew I was there. He...' Jan paused, shaking her head impatiently. 'This is quite ridiculous! There's nothing between us. We've barely even met!'

'It was obvious the other evening that you shared an attraction,' he declared. 'Each time I looked your way you were smiling at each other. It was the same this evening.'

Jan said flatly. 'That isn't true.'

He drew in a breath. 'You'd have me doubt the evidence of my own eyes?'

'I'd have you not exaggerate what you see out of all proportion,' said Jan, adding with intent, 'Who are you most concerned for, Felipe—yourself or Sabatine?'

He ignored the question. 'I want your word,' he demanded, 'that you won't seek his company again while we are here.'

'I didn't seek it in the first place,' she insisted. 'And I certainly don't intend watching my every step in case I happen to find myself in his proximity again! Perhaps Sabatine should try paying him a little more attention herself. After all, he came as her guest.'

'What Sabatine does or does not do is not your concern.' His tone was implacable. '*You* will do as I say!'

Jan set her own jaw. 'Not if what you say is irrational. I'm an individual, Felipe. I have the right to say no to you if and when I choose!'

His eyes smouldered. 'As my wife, you have no rights other than those I care to grant you. When will you learn that?'

'When hell freezes over!' She was too incensed herself to heed any warning signals. 'You may have forced this marriage on us both, but you can't force me to accept your superiority!'

'I've never used force with you.' His voice had gone silky soft, and all the more dangerous for it. 'That was my mistake. I should have taught you who was master from the outset.'

Jan took an involuntary step backwards as he reached for her, but she was too late to stop the long, lean fingers from seizing the front of her dress. There came the sound of ripping fabric as both side-seams split, then the narrow shoulder-straps gave way and the whole garment sagged to the floor.

Because of the heat, she was wearing nothing beneath but a pair of thin silk briefs. Felipe dealt with those in the same manner, tossing the remnants contemptuously aside before dragging her up into his arms to press a savage kiss on her mouth.

She was too stricken to fight. She doubted, in any case, if she could have prevailed against his strength. He was hurting her in more ways than the one, his hands roaming her body with ruthless intent, his anger over-riding all bounds of consideration.

When he swung her on to the bed she lay there like a log while he stripped off his clothing. Looking into the ruthless features as he came over her, she remembered the first time he had taken her—the patience and gentleness he had shown in arousing her. This time he obviously didn't care how or what she felt.

'Don't,' she whispered, the plea dragged from her against her will. 'Not like this!'

His expression didn't alter. Use came suddenly back to her limbs. Both hands doubled into fists, she beat at the broad shoulders, twisting beneath him in an effort to escape the heady torment he was inflicting. He didn't even lift his head, simply shifted his grip to seize both her wrists and pin them down to the pillows on either side of her head. She was helpless beneath his weight, unable to stir a muscle.

It was over quickly. He didn't linger, rolling away from her without a word. Throat dry and aching, Jan lay where he had left her. Sabatine was responsible for this, she thought numbly. Felipe had used her as a release for his frustrated desires, that was all. Everything else had been an excuse.

'I hate you,' she whispered, and meant it with all her heart at that moment. 'You're despicable!'

'I'm your husband,' he gritted. 'I won't have you defy me!'

'And this was supposed to make me respect you?' Her laugh jarred. 'You have a lot to learn about English women!'

It was a moment or two before he responded to that. When he did speak, it was on a controlled note. 'We both of us have much to learn, it seems. But learn we must, because there is no changing the situation.'

He would change his mind if she failed to fulfil her side of the contract, Jan reflected bitterly. They had nothing else to hold them together. Not any more.

CHAPTER EIGHT

THE bullring was smaller than she had anticipated. Walls of white stone enclosed the area, with the occasional wooden *burladero* inside to provide protection.

Faced by men on heavily padded horses, each young bull released from the pens was judged on its response to the challenge. Only those displaying the proper spirit were kept, the rejects set aside to be raised as beef cattle. Either way, Jan reflected, it came to the same thing in the end.

'Why is all the testing done from horseback?' she asked Domingo, who was viewing proceedings along with his guests.

'Because the bull that takes part in the *corrida* must never until that moment have seen a man on foot,' he replied. 'This is why it charges the cape, because the cape is moving.' He cast her a glance, the aristocratic features unbending a little. 'Felipe has not yet taken you to a *corrida*?'

Jan bit back the comment that sprang to her lips. Domingo was her host. It would be impolite, to say the least, to state her views in his hearing. 'There hasn't really been time yet,' she said instead.

'No.' This time his glance held a certain appraisement. 'You are learning to adjust to our ways?'

Her smile felt stiff. 'Some of them.'

'It is never easy for two people from differing cultures to form a true understanding,' he said. 'You must acquire tolerance.'

Perhaps fortunately, he didn't give her chance to respond to that statement, turning to answer some
comment from the man on his other side. Jan gazed into
the ring where the last of the young bulls was being lured
back to the pen. It was all very well to talk about tolerance, but last night had been beyond all limits. Felipe
had been icily polite all morning—as if she and not he
were at fault. Even now he was avoiding her, standing
over there with a couple of other men. At least Sabatine
wasn't hanging around him at the moment. Not that she
wasn't welcome to him, anyway!

There was a short lull after the ring was cleared. A
general air of anticipation ran through the audience as
the door leading to the bull-pens was opened once more.
Small though it might be by *corrida* standards, the animal
that erupted into the ring was menacing enough in its
black presence. Coming to an abrupt halt, it stood for
a moment getting its bearings, head swinging from side
to side as mingled scents reached its nostrils, horns
curving to razor-sharp points.

Felipe had disappeared. The sight of him entering the
ring from the far side, the *muleta* ready in his hand,
brought Jan's heart into her mouth. For all he had said,
she hadn't really expected he would go ahead and do
the thing. He was lean and lithe in the black trousers
and shirt, the scarlet of the cape blown back by the slight
breeze to reveal the yellow lining.

All cattle were colour-blind, Domingo had said earlier;
they would charge as readily at one side of the cape as
the other. So far the bull seemed to be paying little
attention.

With a total lack of caution, or so it appeared to Jan,
the would-be matador walked boldly forward and ges-
tured with the cape. Snorting, the animal pawed with a

front hoof at the ground, then exploded into sudden and terrifying action, crossing the ring with all the speed and thundering purpose of an express train.

To Jan's untutored eyes, the skill and grace with which Felipe guided the bull past his body was nothing short of miraculous. The horn tip must have come within millimetres of his hip! In the following moments he executed several more passes, each one drawing cheers and shouts of encouragement from the assembled audience. Sabatine's expression was exultant. One would have thought, Jan reflected, that she and not Felipe was receiving the accolades. Of those watching, she herself was probably the only one who felt sick with dread for what might happen should he slip or make some mistake. Those horns would disembowel a man as easily as slicing cake!

The relief when he finally stepped behind the protection of the wooden *burladero* was great. For the first time in minutes she was able to draw a deep breath. Finding his adversary vanished on turning from that last pass, the bull commenced to quarter the ring, bellowing a challenge as he went.

'Who goes next?' someone called, to be greeted with general laughter and ribald remarks, but no takers.

Felipe's reappearance signalled another round of applause. Jan steeled herself not to react in any way as Sabatine slid a proprietorial arm through his and smiled up into his eyes.

'*Valeroso!*' she exclaimed, adding something on a softer note that brought a sudden tilt to his lips.

All eyes turned expectantly to Jan, still standing in the same spot. Felipe himself had lost all expression. His face looked carved from stone.

Mouth stiff, she said, 'That was quite a performance.'

The inclination of the dark head held more than a hint of hard mockery. 'I live to fight again some day.'

'We return to the house for luncheon,' announced Carlotta into the slight pause. 'Come.'

Turning to follow the general move, Jan felt her heart jerk as Felipe's hand came down on her shoulder. She could feel the anger in him.

'Did last night teach you nothing of diplomacy?' he demanded softly.

She responded without looking at him. 'Was that what it was supposed to teach me?'

His sigh was barely audible. 'You drive me to such measures.'

'Because I refuse to sit back and allow you to dictate my every action?' she asked recklessly. 'Where I come from respect has to be earned, not taken as a due. Getting into the ring with that bull did nothing to enhance your masculine image. Not, at least, in my eyes. I have more respect for those who didn't.' It was sheer malice that made her add, 'Like Luis, for instance. He obviously doesn't feel the need to prove himself.'

The others had already reached the small fleet of cars that had brought them out from the house. Felipe's grasp had tightened painfully for a moment, now it relaxed again, although he didn't remove the hand. 'I haven't yet begun to prove myself,' he said grimly, propelling her forward. 'Be warned.'

Lunch was an informal affair eaten al fresco. During the course of the afternoon, one or two people slipped away to embrace siesta in the privacy and peace of their rooms, leaving the rest to while away the time in desultory conversation. Jan chose to go for the simple reason that staying was too much of an effort, not that she was particularly weary.

Lying on the bed in the dim coolness, she considered a future devoid of reassurance. Felipe's threat hadn't been an idle one. He wouldn't be satisfied until he had her under total control. Given other circumstances, she might have been able to bring herself to accept his dictum to a certain extent, but whatever it was she still felt for him, it didn't go deep enough to merit that kind of self-sacrifice. She would fight, and go on fighting, to retain some individuality.

Or leave him, came the thought. Now, while there was still time.

Only was there? Conception could have taken place last night, for all she knew. Even if it hadn't, Felipe would never allow her to just walk away from it all. Not, at least, until he had lost all hope of achieving his aim through her.

By four o'clock she could lie still no longer. On the other hand, she had no desire to join the party downstairs again just yet. She went out on to the balcony, thankful to find it empty, as was indeed the courtyard below.

The heat had begun to wane. Drawing in a breath of the sultry air, she caught the scent from the geraniums massed in planters about the perimeter. There came the sound of a chair being scraped over stone almost immediately beneath her feet, followed by the chink of a glass replaced on one of the marble-topped tables. Whoever was down there was seated under the canopy formed by the balcony, and hidden from view from above, but the voice when it came carried well enough.

Felipe spoke in Spanish, his tone measured. 'There is no use in regret.'

'It isn't too late.' Sabatine's own tone was soft, the words difficult to catch. 'If you get rid of her, I'll give you a child myself.'

There was a pause. When Felipe spoke again it was on the same flat, unemotional note. 'You have no desire to bear a child.'

Listening, rooted to the spot, Jan could almost sense the dismissive shrug. 'I was perhaps too hasty in that decision. It would be but a few months' discomfort.' Her voice softened again persuasively. 'We are meant for each other, Felipe. You know this. She can never be the wife you need.'

Jan waited to hear no more. Moving silently, she went back into the bedroom. Suspecting the way Felipe still felt about Sabatine was one thing, hearing it confirmed from his own lips something else again. If he'd been content to bide his time a little, he could probably have had everything he wanted. Lacking in true mothering instinct though Sabatine still appeared to be, who was to say that she would have remained indifferent to her own child? And even if she had, would he have cared?

Hypothetical questions to which there could be no answer, she acknowledged numbly. Felipe had married her, Jan. That was inescapable fact. Even if he gave in to Sabatine's pleas and got rid of her, that wouldn't dissolve the marriage. With no idea at all of the Spanish law regarding divorce, she couldn't be sure how long it might take, but it was hardly going to be an overnight process, whatever.

She was changed from the trousers and shirt she had worn that morning into a simple linen skirt and matching blouse when Felipe finally put in an appearance around five o'clock.

'You slept?' he queried, studying her averted face. 'You look far from rested.'

'I dreamed about home,' she said with some deliberation. '*My* home, not yours.'

'This is your home now,' he responded hardily. 'You must forget about the other.'

She turned on him then, eyes full of fire. 'You can't govern my thoughts—or my feelings, either. I despise you, Felipe! You have no honour.'

The muscles around his mouth went white, his fists curling at his sides. For a moment he seemed almost on the verge of hitting her, then he brought himself under control with a visible effort.

'Perhaps to a degree I deserve that,' he said tautly, 'so I'll let it pass.'

He was in the bathroom with the door closed between them before Jan could bring herself to move. She had contemplated facing him with the conversation she had overheard, but the words had remained locked inside her. What difference could it make, anyway? She had never been under any illusions regarding her role in his life.

They left the ranch at four the following afternoon. Driving away, Jan was glad to see the back of the place. At the very least, she would be free of the too observant eyes, the effort needed to keep up any semblance of normality.

Felipe had made no attempt to come near her last night. He was remote again, locked into his own thoughts. Sabatine's goodbye had been said in private— or so Jan assumed. There had been no sign of her on their departure, although Luis had been in view. Whether

Felipe had said anything to him, Jan couldn't be sure, but he had certainly seemed to be steering clear.

As before, the seed bulls were sheltering from the heat under their individual trees, black hides melting into the shadows. The sight of a group of people seated on a grassy knoll in one of the enclosures, with blue and white picnic cloth spread out, brought the car to a sharp halt in a cloud of dust as Felipe applied the brakes.

He was out of the vehicle before Jan could move a muscle, crossing swiftly to the fence to call something she couldn't quite catch. Lifting a hand complete with beer bottle, one of the young men waved cheerfully back.

'*No comprendo,*' he called in an unmistakable accent.

'I asked,' Felipe repeated, switching to English, 'if you had looked over there beneath the trees before you climbed the fence?'

'Oh, you mean the old boy having a siesta?' He sounded unconcerned. 'We're not bothering him.'

'At the moment, apparently not,' Felipe agreed drily. 'When you begin to repack your belongings it may well be another matter. I'd advise you to leave both basket and cloth and make your escape while the going, as you would say, is good.'

'Oh, come on!' said one of the two girls on a derisive note. 'You're just trying to frighten us, aren't you? The animal hasn't moved in half an hour!'

'All the same,' put in her companion with a suddenly nervous glance towards the subject under discussion, 'I think we should pack up and go. We're probably trespassing, anyway.'

'There's no "probably" about it.' Felipe's patience was wearing thin. 'If the bull charges it will be no one's fault but your own.'

The other girl laughed. 'It doesn't have enough energy to charge anything. Anybody can see that!' Leaping to her feet, she snatched up the cloth, heedless of the picnic remains scattering about her. Parodying a matador, she held the material at arm's length and shook it invitingly in the bull's direction. '*Olé*, then!'

Out of the car herself by now, Jan saw the massive bulk stir into sudden and startling life. One moment it was just standing there, the next thundering out into the open, horns glinting in the sunlight like devil's wings. Felipe was over the fence in what looked like a single bound, and running to snatch the cloth from the girl's hands.

'Get out of here, all of you!' he shouted. 'Now!'

None of the four paused to pick anything up. Hand to mouth, Jan watched the bull bear down on the man still wielding the blue and white cloth. He was going to draw it off—give the others time to get over the fence to safety. But then how would he himself get away unscathed? There was no *burladero* here to take shelter behind.

The first pass was so close, man and bull seemed to meld together. This animal was almost twice the size of the two-year-old he had caped the day before; twice as dangerous, too, to judge from the speed and concentrated ferocity of its turn and renewed attack. Jan held her breath as the great head hooked savagely to the right, but Felipe somehow miraculously avoided impalement, leading the animal through, then immediately dropping the cloth to spring for the fence before the bull could make a second turn.

He made it with bare seconds to spare, vaulting the five-foot height to land with bone-jarring force in the dust of the narrow roadway.

Snorting, the bull made a half-hearted attack on the fence itself, but it was only for show. The trespassers had been routed, its territory was once more its own. Nevertheless, it remained there pawing the ground and glaring, daring them to try it again.

The four tourists looked anything but comfortable.

'Thanks,' proffered the second of the two young men gruffly. 'We just didn't realise there was any danger.'

'You were wonderful!' exclaimed the girl clinging to his arm, eyeing Felipe in admiration. 'Are you a matador?'

Still breathing harshly from the exertion, he ignored the question. 'Never,' he advised, 'take anything for granted where animals are concerned. They have their own code of rules.'

'What about our things?' asked the girl who had provoked the attack, on a subdued note. 'It isn't even our basket.'

Her partner said it for them all. 'If you want to go back in there and get it, go right ahead! We'll have to replace it, that's all. Lucky we left the rest of our gear in the car.'

Felipe came back to where Jan stood, his face expressionless as he met her eyes. She slid into her seat, still too shocked by the speed of the whole episode to make any comment. As they pulled away, the chastened quartet were getting into their own vehicle, abandoning basket, cloth and what remained of their meal to the sentinel still standing guard at the fence.

'I imagine,' Jan ventured after a moment or two, 'that there might be some consternation when those things are found.'

'There would be even more,' Felipe replied grimly, 'if four bodies accompanied them. It will be assumed that someone had a lucky escape, that's all. It isn't the first time tourists have mistaken somnolence for docility. Being so close to the coast, the Murillo pastures attract many a passing party.'

'There's plenty of unfenced land,' Jan observed. 'You'd think they'd have the sense to stick to it!'

'Any form of barrier is a challenge to some mentalities.' His lips were compressed. 'Perhaps they'll think twice next time.'

He was silent after that. Jan stole the occasional glance, struck by a certain rigidity of muscle in his jawline. Was this how it was to be between them from now on? she wondered dully. Was his yearning for the woman he had left behind so great that he couldn't even put up a pretence any longer?

'You were very courageous back there,' she said at length, desperate for something—anything—to break the atmosphere. 'That creature was even more savage than the one you fought yesterday.'

'He was older,' came the dry response, 'and therefore more tetchy. It was necessary to do something. There was no time to be afraid.'

She said softly, 'I didn't think you knew what fear was.'

'Because I choose to test myself in ways you don't understand?' He shrugged. 'You preferred to see it as what you would term "showing off", I believe?' He cast a glance her way when she failed to answer, mouth sardonic. 'Isn't that so?'

'If you really want to know, then yes, I suppose I did,' she responded stiffly. 'You could have been killed!'

'And where would that have left you? Was *that* your concern?'

'No!' The denial came fierce. 'I couldn't care less about how I stand as your widow. I want nothing of yours!'

'A foolish attitude, but no more than I'd expect from you. Your pride is misplaced, *querida*.'

It had been some time since he had last used that form of endearment; it wasn't, she told herself, meant as such now. 'My pride——' she began, then stopped abruptly as she saw the flicker of pain cross his features. 'Felipe? Are you hurt?'

'It's nothing,' he denied. 'Just a scratch.'

She ran her eyes down the side visible to her, breath catching in her throat as she saw the jagged tear in his trousers, the spreading dark patch at the top of his thigh. 'That's more than just a scratch! Why didn't you say?'

His lips twisted. 'To what purpose? I'll have Dr Valdes take a look at it when we're home.'

'The way you're bleeding, it can't possibly wait that long!' Jan peeled off the white cotton jacket she was wearing, wadding it into a thick pad and applying pressure to the general area. 'Chiclana is closer. There must be a doctor there.'

'You make too much of it,' he protested.

'So, all right, indulge me for once.' She was determined not to give way. 'There's nothing wrong in playing safe.'

His sigh held resignation. 'If you insist.'

'I do.' Then she added quickly, 'Better, too, if I drove, then you can hold the pad yourself.'

Already the cloth was turning scarlet. Felipe eased his position, his jaw tensing again momentarily. 'I wasn't aware you could drive.'

'I have talents I haven't even discovered myself yet.' She kept her tone light, failing to add that she had passed her test in England just a matter of days before coming here. The more he used that leg, the more he pumped blood out of the wound. She knew enough to keep the car on the road at least.

The change-over was made without incident, except that the cloth became redder than ever. Before setting off again, Jan rooted through her bag in the back to come up with the towelling swim-robe she had thrown in when she had discovered there was a pool at the ranch. Felipe made no protest when she handed it to him.

'I'm afraid,' he said wryly, 'that your jacket is ruined.'

'You can always buy me another,' she responded, sliding behind the wheel.

With a silent prayer for the ability to handle the unfamiliar vehicle, she turned the key in the ignition. The transmission was automatic, thank heaven. Gear changing she could live without.

The first half-mile was the worst. She was just beginning to get the feel of the car when they hit the main coastal road. Her heart sank like a stone when she saw the amount of traffic heading towards Cádiz, but there was nothing else for it. At least she didn't have to cross the nearside stream in this country to turn right.

Waiting her chance, she pulled out, increasing speed to match the vehicle in front. Chiclana was just a few kilometres ahead. They should reach it in fifteen minutes or so. Felipe had his head back against the rest, his eyes closed. A film of perspiration beaded his upper lip. Don't die! she thought wildly. Please, don't die!

Surrounded by olive groves and vineyards, the town sported a massive eighteenth century church. It was in one of the narrow streets behind it that, following directions given by a passer-by, she finally found what she sought. At this hour on a Sunday afternoon there was no surgery, of course, but the doctor lived right next door to his place of work. Only when she had made sure he was at home and willing to treat the patient could she begin to relax a little.

By British standards, the surgery was bare to the point of austerity, but it looked clean enough. There was an examination couch in one corner. Felipe lay down on it with some reluctance.

Sodden from hip to knee by now, the brown trousers were not worth saving. Dr Mendoza lost no time in taking a pair of scissors to slash open the whole leg.

Watching from the other side of the table, Jan was unable to stifle her exclamation when she saw the extent of the damage. The gash was some six inches in length, running across the front of the muscled thigh about an inch below the groin. Blood welled from it with every breath Felipe took.

'Press here with the palm of your hand,' the doctor instructed Jan, indicating a spot high up on the inner thigh. 'I must fetch instruments.'

Felipe's face looked grey, the lines deeply etched, but he was still able to raise a mocking brow as she brought pressure to bear.

'You've nothing to fear from me at the moment. I am, as you see, indisposed.'

'Shut up,' she hissed furiously, afraid that the doctor might understand English. 'This is neither the time nor the place!'

The man returned carrying a kidney dish containing the necessary items. A tourniquet was applied, releasing Jan from her task. She stood back while the wound was cleaned and stitched.

'Where did you cape the bull that did this?' asked the doctor at one point.

'How did you know it was a bull?' queried Jan when Felipe showed no immediate response.

The smile was brief. 'I have seen many such wounds in my time. Your husband is fortunate to have escaped more serious injury.'

'I'm no professional,' Felipe said shortly. 'This was an accident.'

He lay back then, as if the few words had exhausted him, leaving Jan to supply a fuller explanation.

'They should have been left to suffer the consequences of their foolishness,' pronounced her listener judiciously when she finished the tale. He tied the last knot, straightening with a sigh. 'That is the best I can do. Care should be taken not to reopen the wound.'

Felipe made an attempt to sit up, the remaining colour draining from his face as he did so. The doctor shook his head.

'You have lost a great deal of blood. There should be a transfusion.'

Jan said swiftly, 'Can you do that here?'

'I have the equipment, but not the blood itself,' he acknowledged. 'You must go to the hospital.' He looked back to where his patient still sat on the edge of the couch, fighting the dizziness that was obviously threatening to overtake him. 'Do you know your blood type?'

The answer was slow in coming. 'A Negative.'

'Not a common group,' on a note of concern. 'It is doubtful if any but Sevilla will have it readily available.'

Jan could hardly get the words out. 'I'm A Negative, too!'

Both men were gazing at her. The doctor was the first to break the silence. 'You are quite sure of this?'

'Oh, yes. I've been a donor for two years. They gave me a card to carry.' She was still scarcely able to believe the coincidence herself. 'The blood tests I had in my medical proved that my blood is OK. What about a direct transfusion?'

'That is no problem,' he agreed. 'Although no more than the standard amount, of course.' To Felipe, he added, 'You will make up any balance yourself in a few days.'

The latter's eyes were on Jan, his expression difficult to define. 'You don't have to do this,' he said.

She looked back at him steadily. 'It's necessary.'

For lack of a second couch, she was seated on a chair at his side. Dr Mendoza set up the apparatus deftly enough, and with creditable asepsis. Watching the transparent tubing, Jan saw her own blood begin to flow, following it with her eyes to the point where it disappeared under the bandage that held the needle in Felipe's arm. It gave her an odd sensation, as if a part of her life-force were being drawn from her.

Felipe said quietly, 'I owe you a great deal, Janita. But for your insistence on bringing me here, I might well have suffered far more serious consequences—to say nothing of this.'

Gratitude was the last thing she wanted from him, but apparently all she was going to get. She hardened her heart against the shaft of pain. 'No more than I'd do for anyone,' she returned on an umemotional note. 'Lucky we happened to be the same blood group.'

His lips slanted. 'A chance in a million, Valdes told me.'

'You knew?'

'Of course. I was given the results of all the tests he made.' His eyes were on her face, twin mirrors in which she could see her own reflection. 'The gypsies would call it fate.'

The gypsies, she thought bitterly, didn't know what they were talking about—at least, one of them didn't. A long life together with contentment at the end of it. How wrong could anyone be? She might eventually become the mother of his son and heir, but that was all she would ever really mean to him. Could she face that kind of future?

CHAPTER NINE

DR MENDOZA insisted Jan herself rested for at least twenty minutes after the transfusion was completed. It would, he advised, be better for them both if they stayed the night right here in Chiclana and continued their journey in the morning after a good night's sleep.

'I would prefer my own bed,' declared Felipe unequivocally. 'If you will allow me the use of your telephone, I will arrange our transportation.'

'I can drive us,' Jan protested. 'I got this far!'

'With more luck than expertise,' came the dry response. 'Juan and Carlos will come.'

To argue the point would not only be futile but foolish, she conceded. It would be dark soon, and she had no experience at all of night driving. All the same, she felt slighted.

Clad in fresh trousers fetched in from the car, Felipe looked almost his normal self again. Only in the occasional drawing together of his brows as he moved was there any evidence of discomfort.

The doctor took them next door to his home and had his wife supply coffee while they waited. Felipe's name on the cheque with which he settled the bill brought instant and deferential recognition. The attention of the family physician should be sought at first opportunity, he instructed, not about to be accused of encroaching on another's territory. He would take out the stitches when the time came. For the present, it was essential to proceed with caution if the wound was not to reopen.

Stiffened though the leg had obviously become by the time Juan and Carlos arrived, Felipe refused assistance out to the car. He spoke little on the way back to the *hacienda*, but there was no disguising the strain about his mouth and eyes when they hit a rough patch of road. By rights he should be in hospital, Jan thought. The wound had gone deep; who was to tell if Dr Mendoza's surgical skill had been adequate to the demands made on it?

He was forced to sink his pride and accept help on reaching the house, because he wouldn't have got out of the car at all without it. Once safely upstairs, however, he dismissed Juan and made the bedroom under his own steam, with Jan following resignedly in his wake.

'Who was it who told me not so very long ago that *my* pride was misplaced?' she asked from the doorway as he lowered himself to a seat. 'No one's going to think any the worse of you if you show a little human weakness.'

'I'm not an invalid,' he responded doggedly. 'In a day or two I'll prove it to you.'

'I suppose,' she said with unconcealed sarcasm, 'I should be relieved you're allowing yourself that much recovery time. Dr Valdes may have other ideas.'

'He's my advisor, not my mentor. I know my own limitations.'

'Do you? I'm not so sure.' She changed her tack, aware that she was getting precisely nowhere, moving forward to add appealingly, 'At least rest the leg for now. We can have dinner up here—that's if you feel like eating?'

'Such concern,' he mocked. 'But then no more than you'd feel for anyone, of course. Yes, I require food. I have to keep up my strength—if only to fulfil my marital obligations.'

It was hopeless, Jan acknowledged wryly. He would go his own way regardless of what advice was offered. 'Pig-headed' was the word, though hardly one he would appreciate. He had come within an ace of losing the masculinity that meant so much to him, and she had been witness. For that reason alone he would allow himself no further weakness in her sight.

Despite being brought up on trays, dinner was still a lavish affair. Jan found herself surprisingly hungry once she got down to it. Making up for the blood she had lost, she assumed.

Felipe disappeared into the bathroom shortly after they had finished eating, to emerge some twenty minutes later wearing a robe and the bottom half of blue silk pyjamas. Still damp, his hair testified to the shower he had taken. He looked drawn, Jan thought, but she bit back any comment to that effect.

The bottle of pain-killers Dr Mendoza had supplied was standing where she had put it on one of the glass shelves. Whether any were gone was difficult to say, when she wasn't certain how many there had been to start with. If he showed no inclination to send for Dr Valdes she would do it herself, she vowed. All very well being stoic about things but, left unattended, anything could happen to that wound.

Pain-killers or no, he was in bed and already asleep when she finally went back. She stood for several moments studying the face outlined against the whiteness of the pillow. By lamplight his skin looked almost too tautly stretched, the bone structure sharply defined. A comma of dark hair had fallen across his forehead. Without thinking about it, Jan put out a hand and gently brushed it back, lingering with the crisp thickness beneath her fingers. In this man's arms she had run the whole gamut of emotion. Right now she wasn't sure what it was she felt—only that it made her all churned up inside.

He stirred restlessly, murmuring something she couldn't quite catch. She moved abruptly away. Whoever he was dreaming about, it wouldn't be her.

Apart from a certain stiffness when he walked, he showed little sign of any aftermath the next day, she was bound to admit. She felt both tired and listless herself, but that was more of a mental than a physical *malaise*.

His announcement at breakfast that he would be going in to the winery as usual she accepted with resignation.

'I gather Juan will be driving you in,' she said.

The denial was short and sharp. 'I'm quite fit now to drive myself.'

Jan clamped down on the protest. What was the use? 'You'll be back to lunch?' was all she allowed herself.

'It's doubtful,' he said. 'The harvesting began at sunrise.' He looked at her with hooded eyes. 'You don't wish to be alone?'

She shrugged. 'I dare say I can find something to occupy my mind.'

'Without a doubt.' He finished his coffee and pushed back his chair, the irony just visible in the tilt of his upper lip. 'There are many good books in the library.'

Take care, it was on the tip of her tongue to call after him as he went from the room, but she caught herself up in time. He wanted no solicitude from her.

The day stretched ahead of her, long and hot and devoid of appeal. Her life here was aimless—at present, anyway. She tried to imagine what it might be like with a baby to look after, but the image refused to jell. One thing was certain, if she did become a mother there would be no nannies to take over from her.

She went out to the pool and swam for a while, but the exercise did little to ease her depression. Leda's telephone call around ten-thirty made a welcome break. Apparently she had happened to phone through last night just after Juan and Carlos had left for Chiclana, and been given the news of Felipe's injury. She was anxious to know his condition.

'He is foolish!' she declared when Jan told her where he was. 'Why must men always prove themselves this way? You must insist that he see his own physician, Janita. One cannot be too careful with such an injury.'

Jan's laugh sounded brittle even to her ears. 'Since when did a Rimados listen to advice from a mere woman?'

There was a pause before Leda answered, her tone suddenly altered, 'It has been known. Are you well yourself, Janita?'

Jan pulled herself together with an effort. 'I'm fine. Just feeling the heat, that's all.'

'Another month and it will begin to grow cooler.'

Another month? She couldn't see that far ahead. This marriage of theirs was deteriorating daily, it seemed. How did she get through the next week, never mind the next month?

More than ever at a loose end after Leda had rung off, she thought suddenly of the two cars still left in the garages. If she could drive under the kind of pressure she had experienced yesterday, she could surely manage to get as far as Jerez without running into any trouble. There were one or two small items she could do with replacing, and it would give her a chance to get to know the place a little better. She could even have lunch out—perhaps at some small, obscure place where no one would know who she was. Anything was better than just sitting around here waiting for Felipe to get back.

She chose a simple white cotton dress as the least likely to draw attention, clipping her hair back from her face with a couple of slides and leaving her skin free of make-up apart from a dab of lipstick. An ordinary holiday-maker, she thought in satisfaction, viewing her reflection before leaving the room. For this one day she was going to forget her problems and play the tourist to the hilt.

The first drawback came in the realisation that she didn't have keys to either car. Juan looked a little perturbed when she sought him out to ask where they might be kept.

'Don Felipe left no instructions,' he said.

'I doubt if he'd consider it necessary,' Jan returned firmly. 'I'll take the Mercedes, I think.'

The keys were handed over with some reluctance. No doubt he would be telling his master of her excursion, but by then it would be too late. She had to get out, if only for a few hours. Just to be herself again without a care in the world!

The pickers were hard at work beneath the hot sun, moving steadily along the rows of vines with their baskets. Only when the grapes were deposited on the truck waiting to transport them to the winery would automation take over. Judging from the size and quantity of fruit on every vine, it was going to be a bumper harvest.

Jan wondered fleetingly if she would still be here for the next one, then dismissed the thought. One day at a time was going to be her maxim from now on.

The town was crowded. She left the car parked in a side street, and made her way to the main shopping area.

There were still a couple of hours to go before siesta closed many places down. Time enough then to think about lunch, if she was hungry enough. Right now it was too hot to think about anything except finding some shade.

It was just after midday when she bumped into Luis. Like her, he was casually dressed. Also like her, he appeared aimless.

'Sabatine has other engagements,' he said when Jan asked the obvious question. 'And Felipe?'

'At the winery.' She added quickly, 'The harvest began today.'

'A busy time,' he agreed. There was a pause, a sudden, almost desperate expression in his eyes. 'Will you allow me to buy you coffee, Janita? I need your advice.'

She was the last person to be asking, Jan reflected ruefully. She couldn't even straighten out her own life. All the same, she found herself nodding. What harm could it do just to listen?

He took her to a small café in the back streets, selecting one of the tables set outside in the tiny square. There was little shade or movement of air. Seated, Jan felt the trickle of perspiration down her back and hoped it wasn't to be too lengthy a discourse.

'I am distraught,' Luis announced without preamble, looking so miserable that she didn't have the heart to smile even inwardly at his choice of words. 'Three times now I have asked Sabatine to be my wife, but still she refuses to give me an answer.'

Jan said cautiously, 'I'm sorry about that, Luis, but I don't really see how I can help.'

'You are a woman,' he said. 'I hoped you may have some insight into her mind.'

If she had, came the thought, it wouldn't be what he wanted to hear. 'We're quite different types,' she said out loud. 'I could no more plumb Sabatine's depths than she could probably plumb mine. Perhaps if you presented her with an ultimatum?'

He lifted his shoulders. 'I have done that already.'

'Obviously not firmly enough. You should set a time limit and stick to it.'

He said doubtfully, 'But perhaps then she would say no simply because I deny her the time to make her decision.'

'Or yes because she doesn't want to risk losing you.' She studied the handsome face for a moment, wondering if he had any insight at all where Sabatine was concerned, or had simply been bowled over by her beauty. 'What does your family think about it?' she asked.

The shrug came again. 'I saw no use in telling them anything until there was something to tell.'

'Are they likely to approve your choice, considering there were such high hopes for a family tie?' she queried with care.

There was an element of a defiance that belied his age in his reply. 'Once they have met her they will understand my feelings. Elena was always too immature for me.'

And Sabatine far too advanced, Jan reflected. It was cruel of her to keep him dangling on a string the way she was doing—although, for Luis's sake, better that than marriage with someone who didn't return the same depth of emotion.

She took her leave after some twenty minutes of fruitless conversation. All Luis had really needed was a sympathetic ear into which to pour his troubles, she told herself ruefully. There was no advice she could have given him, other than to cut his losses and return home, and she doubted whether he was prepared to do that. Anyway, he was old enough to sort out his own life. She had enough on her plate without getting herself involved in someone else's problems.

It was almost one o'clock, and too hot to linger long in the street. She might as well go back to the *hacienda*, she thought disconsolately after studying one or two shop windows. Lunch alone here in town no longer held any appeal.

The traffic had thinned considerably. Enough so to give her more confidence than she had had coming into town. Looking at the street map she had bought earlier, she realised that it would be something of a short cut to drive past the winery on her way home. Not that she intended calling in on Felipe, of course. He would hardly appreciate the gesture.

It was Felipe she was thinking of as she made a right turn at the junction, wondering whether he had contacted Dr Valdes yet. The sudden appearance of another vehicle heading straight for her froze her mind for an instant. It was pure instinct that depressed her foot on the brake and spun the wheel. She felt the bump as her nearside front tyre mounted the kerb, followed by an almighty jolt and the sound of shattering glass as the other car caught her rear end.

In those first few seconds after the engine cut out, she could only sit and stare blindly through the windscreen in total shock. The man who had been driving the other car was the first to reach her, hammering on the window and shouting furious insults regarding women drivers in general. Jan nerved herself to slide down the glass and attempt a stammered apology, but he wasn't in any mood to listen. Turning to the small crowd that had gathered, he appealed for someone to fetch the police while he stood guard over this imbecile tourist who didn't know one side of the street from another.

There must have been a policeman in the vicinity, because one appeared almost immediately. Jan got out of the car at his invitation, holding on to the door for steadiness. Her legs felt like jelly. Still almost beside himself with fury, the other driver gave an account of the accident that was instantly verified by several passers-by. Faced with the knowledge that she had indeed been on the left side of the street instead of the right, Jan had no defence to offer when her turn came, other than to fall back on the tourist theme and hope for the best.

Her English driving licence elicited scant respect. She should, she was informed, be carrying an international licence in order to drive on Spanish roads. She must accompany him, the officer ordered. His companion would bring in her car.

The following minutes were the longest of Jan's life. If there was any relief at all, it was in that the irate driver she had caused to hit her was soon dealt with and sent on his way.

With her maiden name still on the licence, it was necessary to state who she really was, eliciting a change in attitude that was nothing short of miraculous. Don Felipe would be advised of her whereabouts at once, she was told. In the meantime, she must take refreshment to help her recover from her ordeal.

She was drinking coffee in a back room of the station when Felipe was finally ushered in. He looked composed enough on the surface, but Jan could detect anger in the dark eyes.

'You're not hurt in any way?' he asked in English as she came to her feet.

'No,' she assured him. 'I was a bit shaken up, but I'm fine now.' She hesitated, aware of the officer hovering at his back. 'I'm sorry about the car.'

Whether his shrug dismissed the car, her apology or both, she couldn't be sure. 'Come,' he said, 'I'll take you home.'

Seated in the Ferrari at his side, Jan waited until they were clear of the town before venturing to break the silence that lay between them.

'I hope this didn't interrupt anything vital at the winery?'

His lip curled a fraction. 'They're unlikely to run into any trouble if left to their own devices.'

'While I'm not, I suppose,' she responded, bridling at his tone. 'Admittedly the accident was my fault, but it could have happened to anyone unused to driving on the wrong side of the road!'

'It didn't happen to anyone,' he returned shortly, 'it happened to you. You had no authority to take the car at all.'

'I didn't realise I needed permission.' Her tone was frigid. 'You certainly made no objection yesterday!'

'Yesterday I had little other choice. Although, if I'd realised just how inexperienced a driver you were, I might have hesitated.'

'And bled to death while you were doing it!'

The dark head inclined. 'Perhaps so. As today you could have been killed yourself.'

'In which case, you'd simply have had to start all over again with a new candidate for motherhood!'

He cast her a swift glance. 'You believe that to be my only concern?'

'Well, isn't it?' she demanded, and didn't bother to wait for an answer. 'Of course, you could always fall back on Sabatine!'

The strong mouth tautened again. 'You haven't told me yet why you found it necessary to drive into Jerez.'

'Shopping,' she said, and drew another penetrating glance.

'I see no purchases.'

'Window shopping,' she amended lamely. 'I didn't see anything I wanted to buy.'

'You find the town so limited? I must make arrangements to take you to Sevilla again.'

Despite the rush of air created by their speed, Jan felt beaten down by the sheer weight of the sun on the crown of her head. Felipe himself looked affected by the heat for once, his hair clustering damp at the temples. In profile his face had that hawklike quality she had first noted. Was it really only three weeks ago that he had accosted her in the study? It seemed like a lifetime! If Raine had been here in her place, where would she be now? she wondered numbly. Perhaps somewhere out there was a man she could have truly loved and cared for, only she would never know now, would she? Not unless she could free herself of this travesty of a marriage.

Ignoring siesta, the pickers were still hard at work in the vineyard when they passed through. When the harvest was over there would be a great celebration in the village, Yola had said only that morning. This year, she had added slyly, the villagers were hoping for a double cause for celebration. Once her pregnancy was confirmed, her future would be well and truly resolved. If she were going to go at all, it had to be soon—while Felipe was still incapacitated by his injury.

The thought that she might already be caught in that particular trap she pushed to the back of her mind, where it could do least harm.

Advised though the staff had been that neither of them would be in to luncheon, a substantial meal was readily provided within fifteen minutes of their arrival. Jan forced herself to eat, although it was the last thing she felt like doing. Felipe himself seemed to have little appetite. He looked drawn about the eyes. She wanted to ask him if he were in any pain, but doubted if he would admit to it, anyway. If he lacked the sense to see Dr Valdes, then there was little she could do. He certainly wouldn't thank her for any interference.

He retired to the study immediately after they finished the meal. Left to her own devices again, Jan changed and went out to the pool. Swimming at least cooled her body.

Afterwards, she lay on one of the loungers under an opened umbrella, and tried to sort out her priorities. Life here was becoming intolerable. She didn't think she could take much more. Leaving Felipe was her only hope, even though it would mean using the money she had sworn not to touch. Getting Raine to return the rest wouldn't be easy, in any case. In all probability, it was already spent. Even facing her at all was going to be difficult, considering the circumstances.

So go somewhere else, came the thought. Cut out the past altogether and start afresh. With five thousand pounds to her credit she could pick and choose. Scotland might be an idea. Felipe would be unlikely to look for her there.

The thought of never seeing him again brought a sudden hard lump to her throat. Given any incentive at all, she could have made something of this marriage.

Only not with Sabatine constantly in the background. That went beyond the grain. Let her be the one to provide Felipe with an heir.

Eyes closed against the glare penetrating even the heavy cotton, she became aware of some other presence, opening them to find Felipe himself materialised at her side. His face was hard-set, his eyes as black as pitch.

'You lied to me,' he stated grimly. 'You went to Jerez this morning to meet with Luis Fernández!'

Her immediate response was unstudied. 'Who told you?' Realising the implication, she made hasty adjustment. 'It wasn't like that!'

His lip curled. 'What exactly are you denying?'

'That the meeting was arranged.' She came upright on the lounger, curling one arm about her bent knees for support. 'I had no idea Luis was going to be in town.'

'You were seen taking lunch with him.'

'Coffee.' She was trying to stay cool and calm about it. 'We met by chance and he invited me to have a cup of coffee with him.'

His expression showed no sign of relaxing. 'To what purpose?'

'A simple matter of courtesy; that's all. Surely there's nothing wrong in drinking coffee in broad daylight? We only spent half an hour together—if that.'

'And talked of what?'

Jan's lips compressed. 'Nothing that need concern you.'

The skin about his mouth whitened visibly as his teeth came together. 'I'll be the judge of that.'

'No, you won't!' Her voice came out like a whip-crack. 'Whatever Luis said to me was in confidence, and that's how it's going to remain.'

Felipe bent and pulled her roughly to her feet, holding her there in front of him with fingers digging into her shoulders. 'You'll tell me what is between the two of you,' he gritted.

His anger was frightening, but she refused to be cowed by it. Blue eyes blazed back at him. 'There's nothing between us! Luis is a friend. I'm allowed friends, aren't I?'

'Friend?' The tone was scathing. 'You expect me to believe the relationship purely platonic?'

'I don't care what you believe,' she said recklessly, goaded by the sheer injustice of the accusation. 'I'm sick of your attitude, Felipe—sick of you, if it comes to that! I can't bear you near me!'

There was a hint of cruelty in the curl of his lip. 'That is unfortunate.'

His mouth was ruthless. Jan felt herself suffocating beneath the pressure, violated by the vicious thrust of his tongue. She struggled wildly as his fingers found the clasp of her bikini top, tearing herself free to gasp. 'The servants!'

There was a moment when he didn't appear to be taking any notice, then he brought himself sharply under control. Eyes glittering, he said thickly, 'I agree this is not the place. So we go indoors.'

The hand grasping her upper arm was like a tourniquet. Jan could feel her fingers going numb. She stumbled on the pathway leading to the house, and Felipe jerked her upright again with a scant regard for any pain he might be causing her. He was limping a little himself, she realised, but was obviously not about to let his injury deter him from his purpose.

'This isn't going to solve anything,' she got out. 'Don't make me hate you any more than I already do, Felipe!'

His laugh was low and raw. 'It makes little difference to me. You're here to fulfil a purpose—or had you forgotten?'

The transition from bright hot sunlight to the cool dimness of the house was some small relief, the sight of Leda Fuente standing in the hall with Juan a greater one. Why she was here was of secondary importance at the moment. What mattered was that she *was* here. Felipe came to an abrupt halt, the hand holding Jan's arm dropping from her.

'Has something happened to Gaspar?' he asked in swift and sudden concern.

Leda shook her head, her expression uncertain as her gaze went from him to Jan and back again. 'No, he is quite well. We were concerned about you, Felipe. Gaspar agreed I should come to see for myself how you are.'

The answering smile was brief. 'I am, as you see, quite fit, but the gesture is appreciated.' With scarcely a pause, he added, 'I'm afraid I must return to the winery, but Janita will welcome your company. You will, of course, be staying overnight?'

Expression composed now, thoughts well-hidden, she said, 'That was my intention. Shall I see you this evening?'

'At dinner,' he promised, and went without a further glance in Jan's direction.

CHAPTER TEN

JAN was the first to break the silence. She avoided direct confrontation with the questioning eyes opposite.

'It will only take me a few minutes to dress. Yola usually brings me afternoon tea about this time. Would you like some yourself, Leda, or would you prefer something else?'

'Tea will be very suitable,' came the reply. 'I will wait for you out on the patio.'

Upstairs, Jan took a quick shower and got into the first dress that came to hand. A brush over her hair and a dash of lipstick would have to suffice for now. Her face in the mirror looked peaked, her eyes lacklustre. It was over. After this, it had to be over!

Leda looked at her sharply when she emerged from the house, but made no immediate comment. Tea was brought and served. Only after they each had a cup did the Spanish girl broach the subject that was obviously uppermost in her mind.

'Janita, what happened to you and Felipe? I've never seen him look that way before.'

It was past the time for prevarication, Jan conceded wearily. It took a few moments to relate the whole story from the beginning. Leda was silent for several more after she finished. She seemed too stunned to take it in.

'I knew, as I told you, of his original plans concerning your stepsister,' she said at length, 'but I was under the impression that you had changed all that. How could he do such a thing?'

'To be scrupulously fair, I perhaps didn't fight as hard as I might have done,' Jan admitted. 'He's a very... persuasive man.'

'But you don't love him?'

She closed heart and mind against any dissenting voice. 'No.'

There was more sympathy than condemnation in the other girl's eyes. 'Felipe is not the man I thought he was, but he is still our friend. I'll ask Gaspar to speak with him. He must see how wrong he is to act this way.'

'I suppose,' Jan said slowly, 'he did have some reason for anger this afternoon. He thinks I'm having an affair of sorts with another man.'

'And are you?'

'No, but he isn't likely to believe it.' She hesitated. 'Leda, I'd rather you didn't tell Gaspar about this. Not yet, at any rate. It's something I—we have to work out for ourselves.'

The agreement came with reluctance. 'If that is what you want.' She made a helpless little gesture. 'We were so happy for you and Felipe—so convinced that you were right for each other.'

Jan sighed. 'Perhaps I shouldn't have told you.'

'And left me wondering what could possibly have happened in such a short space of time to cause the enmity I saw a little while ago?' Leda shook her head. 'I only wish I could be of some help, but you're right, it's up to the two of you to find yourselves. It will be difficult, but I shall pretend with Felipe that I know nothing of what you've told me.'

She was taking it for granted that something would be worked out in the end, Jan reflected, so why disillusion her any further?

It was almost nine before Felipe returned. Jan had ordered the meal held back until he put in an appearance. When he came downstairs he was wearing the same black silk shirt—or a similar one—that he had worn that very first evening. His skin looked sallow, the lines about his mouth more deeply etched. Tired, Jan thought, steeling her heart against him. Well, he wasn't on his own. She refused to meet his glance, reluctant to see the contempt displayed again. Just a few more days to get through while she made her arrangements, and then goodbye. She only wished she could go right here and now.

For Leda's sake, she made every effort to keep a conversation going throughout the meal. Felipe contributed, but it was obvious that his mind wasn't on what he was saying. He had Juan bring him a double brandy to go with his coffee, and took half of it in a single swallow.

'The humidity is high tonight,' he observed, dabbing his upper lip with his table napkin. 'Let's hope there will be no storm.'

Rain now would ruin the harvest, Jan knew. She didn't think the air particularly heavy herself, but Felipe's lip had already beaded again. The wound was troubling him, that was obvious, yet she couldn't bring herself to broach the subject. Let him suffer! He deserved no better.

Leda herself received short shrift when she ventured to ask if he had seen Dr Valdes as yet. The latter would be taking out the stitches at the proper time, he said. Until then there was nothing to be done.

'Do you have to go back tomorrow?' asked Jan impulsively when the time came to end the evening, reluctant to lose her only confidante. 'Would Gaspar object if you stayed another day?'

Leda shifted her glance fleetingly to Felipe. 'I'm sure not.'

His expression gave nothing away. 'You're more than welcome,' he said. 'But you know that already.'

Jan preceded him up the stairs. Reaching the bedroom, she made a play of shaking out the nightdress laid ready for her across the turned-down coverlet. She didn't want to sleep with Felipe—didn't want him near her—but where else would he allow her to go?

He hadn't moved from the foot of the bed. She could feel his eyes boring into her back, expected any moment to feel his hand yanking her round to face him. His voice when it came was surprisingly restrained.

'Janita, look at me.'

'Why?' Her own voice sounded thick. 'We have already said all there was to say. I'm here for one purpose. Isn't that right?'

'It may have been once. Not any more.' There was a pause, a change of tone. 'I want us to begin again.'

She froze for a moment, then made herself turn to look at him. 'Begin what again?'

'Our whole relationship,' he said. 'I've given you little cause to trust me, I know, but I need you, *querida*.'

She searched the arrogant features with a kind of desperation. 'Trust cuts both ways. Only a few hours ago you believed I was seeing another man.'

'I was jealous,' he admitted. 'The very thought of you with Luis Fernández was anathema to me.' His mouth had a rueful line. 'I arranged our marriage because I wanted to right the wrong I'd done you, yes, but that was only a part of it. I'd never before found a woman I could feel anything deeply for. I'd given up expecting to find one.'

She groped blindly for a seat on the edge of the bed. Her limbs felt weak and trembly, her mind confused. 'You wanted to marry Sabatine,' she got out.

Broad shoulders lifted. 'I realised if I was to produce a son and heir before I was too old to see him reach maturity, it was time I found myself a wife. Sabatine seemed the most suitable choice. When she told me she had no interest in childbearing, I withdrew the offer.'

Jan said slowly, 'She told me *she* refused *you*. You even confirmed it yourself.'

The shrug came again. 'I owed her that much.'

'So what made you think of hiring a surrogate?' she asked baldly.

'Your stepsister first put the idea into my mind,' he admitted. 'Whether she saw herself as candidate initially, I'm not certain, but she showed little hesitation when it came to the point. Then you came along and...' He paused, shaking his head. 'Suffice to say I was blinded by the same need. Love was an emotion I hadn't taken into account.'

A small area of warmth deep inside her was beginning to spread cautious tendrils. 'Why haven't you told me this before?' she whispered.

'Pride,' he acknowledged. 'My Achilles' heel. It was only after I left you this afternoon that I finally realised what it was costing me.' Eyes intent on her face, he added, 'I know I can make you respond to me physically, but I want more than that from you. Do you think you could learn to forget and forgive my past behaviour?'

She swallowed on the dryness in her throat, and said huskily, 'It's going to take time to adjust my ideas, Felipe. Are you really telling me you—love me?'

'Is that so difficult to believe?'

'Yes,' she said. 'Yes, it is. To be honest, I don't think you know what love is.'

'Do you?' he challenged. 'Perhaps we both of us have a great deal to learn about sharing emotion.' He studied her for a moment, his face impassive now. 'Do you hate me so much?'

She shook her head, the hair falling forward to partially hide her face as she looked down at her tightly clasped hands. 'To be honest, I'm not sure what I feel any more.'

'Then perhaps this will help you a little,' he said.

He came forward to draw her to her feet, his hands gentle this time. The kiss held a tenderness she could scarcely believe. She found herself responding to it instinctively, her lips moving blindly beneath his, her body melting against him. He loved her. That was what he had implied. She wanted so much to believe it.

When he put her away from him again she felt bereft. He looked as if he were holding himself deliberately in check.

'This is only confusing the issue,' he declared roughly. 'You have to decide how you feel without any coercion on my part. Tonight we sleep separately. That will give you time to think.' The smile was faint. 'I live in hope.'

Jan stood motionless as he moved away from her. She had wanted his lovemaking—needed the reassurance. Yet he was probably right. In his arms she was incapable of thinking straight; incapable of thinking at all, if it came to that. He wanted more from her than a physical response, he had said. What she had to consider was whether she was capable of giving more.

Sleep was a long time coming. Lying there alone in the bed she tried desperately to sort out her emotions. That she wanted Felipe there was no denying, but wanting was a long way from loving. She wasn't even sure what constituted love.

What it all boiled down to in the end, she supposed, was simple trust. He had sunk his masculine pride to tell her how he felt; surely that fact alone was enough to prove him genuine? 'There is no use in regret', he had said once. In other words, one had to live with one's mistakes. That was advice she might do well to follow herself. Whatever they meant to one another now, it could change and grow in time. All it needed was the opportunity.

Yola awoke her at eight when she brought coffee. The master had already left for the winery, she advised. Whether she realised they had spent the night apart, it was difficult to tell. Not that it mattered, Jan conceded wearily.

Alone again, she sat up and reached for the coffee-cup, her hand faltering as the wave of nausea swept over her. She only just made it to the bathroom, leaning weakly against the bowl afterwards to wipe the back of her hand over her damp forehead and contemplate the dawning probability with mixed emotions.

One bout of morning sickness hardly constituted absolute proof, she tried to tell herself, but, combined with other factors she had failed to take note of, there was little chance of error. Her stomach muscles contracted at the thought of what was even now beginning to take place inside her. A baby. Felipe's child. If there had been any choice before, this had to remove it. She was committed.

She found Leda already at breakfast on the patio when she got down.

'I thought you might be taking the opportunity to lie in for a while,' said the other. 'I understand Felipe left early?'

'Before I woke,' Jan agreed evasively. She sat down at the table, eyeing the coffee-pot and wondering whether she dared risk another try. The nausea had receded, but that wasn't to say it wouldn't return if given any incentive. Leda was too sharp not to guess the reason for her indisposition, and she wasn't yet ready to make any announcement.

'I think I'll stick to orange juice this morning,' she said casually, pouring herself a glass from the vacuumed pitcher. 'Did you sleep well?'

'Not very,' Leda confessed. 'I spent much of the night thinking of what you told me.'

'You mustn't worry about it,' Jan assured her. 'Everything is going to be all right.' And it was, too, she told herself on a sudden surge of confidence. Felipe loved her. What else did she need?

'Then you came to an understanding?' There was an infinite relief in the other girl's expression. 'Felipe needs you, Janita. Far more than perhaps even he fully realises.' She smiled, her whole manner altered. 'I telephoned Gaspar to say I should be staying one more night. So what shall we do with our day?'

'We could drive into town,' Jan suggested, adding hastily, 'In your car, though. I don't have a proper licence yet.'

'Of course.' Leda sounded moɪe than amenable. 'Felipe must take steps to legitimise you.'

He had already done so, Jan reflected, and felt that same warm glow of assurance. She could hardly wait to tell him her news. Tonight they would be together

again—and for the rest of their lives. That prospect was
no longer daunting.

They left the *hacienda* around ten-thirty. Spirits
soaring, Jan felt moved to wave a hand to the nearer
pickers, elated when several waved back.

'They all seem so happy,' she commented. 'Even when
they're toiling in the sun!'

'That's because they have good homes and fair wages,
and know their future is secured now that Don Felipe
has taken himself a wife at last,' Leda responded. 'The
name of Rimados means a lot to your people. Few would
have welcomed the Lobons, should it have come to that
in the end.'

It was on the tip of Jan's tongue to tell her then, but
she held it back. Felipe must be the first to hear it. He
merited no less.

Jerez was thronged with traffic and pedestrians alike.
Sitting back as Leda threaded her way through the streets,
Jan was only too thankful that she wasn't doing the
driving. With practice she would soon become pro-
ficient. Only this time she wouldn't try to run before she
could walk.

The pavement cafés had not yet begun to attract more
than a casual trade. Glancing out of the nearside window
as they paused to allow a group of people to cross the
road, Jan froze at the sight of the man and woman seated
in near solitary state at a table in front of one place of
business. Felipe had his head downbent, his face hidden
from view as he listened to what Sabatine was saying to
him, but even from here she could sense the tension in
him. She felt sick again, her heart heavy as lead.
Whatever the motives behind his declaration last night,
it had meant nothing if he was still seeing the other

woman. She wouldn't share him with Sabatine Valverde.
Not for anything in the world!

'I want to go back,' she said numbly. 'Please, take me
back, Leda. I—I don't feel well.'

Leda wasted no time in obeying. Only when they were
clear of the town again did she speak.

'I saw them, too,' she said. 'But I'm sure you're wrong
in what you are thinking.'

Jan kept her gaze fixed forward. 'I doubt it. If he
can't stay away from her, she can have him!'

Leda glanced at her sharply. 'What are you going to
do?'

'What I should have done long before this. I'm going
home.' She took a steadying breath. 'I have to get my
passport and a few necessities, that's all.'

'You cannot do it!' Leda sounded distressed. 'You
must give Felipe the chance to explain!'

'There's no explanation he can give. They were
together—meeting in secret.'

'Hardly in secret, with all of Jerez to view them.'

'Which just goes to prove how little he cares.' Jan
shook her head. 'It's no use, Leda. I won't be made a
fool of again. I'm going, and you can't stop me!'

There was no reply to that, other than a sigh and a
helpless shrug. Only when they were drawing up at the
house did Leda say tentatively, 'How do you intend to
leave?'

'By air, if I can get to Seville.' Jan gave her an oblique
glance. 'I know it's asking a lot, but will you drive me
there?'

The sigh came again. 'I can't do that.'

'So I'll have to take the estate wagon. It can be picked
up later.'

'But you have no licence to drive!'

'I'll just have to take the chance.'

Jan slid from the car and made her way indoors. Felipe still had her passport, but it had to be in the house. She went to the study and began searching the desk-drawers. The top right-hand one was locked. Snatching up a paper-knife, she prised it open. Her passport lay on top of the paper she had signed that fateful morning. What a gullible, trusting little fool she had been! Only not any more. Not ever again!

Without bothering to read it through, she took the contract and tore it into tiny pieces, scattering them over the desk-top. Leda watched her from the doorway in some bewilderment.

'What are you doing?' she asked.

'Just tidying up some loose ends.' Passport in hand, Jan moved towards the door, meeting the other girl's pleading eyes with no lessening of resolve. 'I'm sorry, Leda. I just can't stay here any longer.'

The Spanish girl followed her to the stairs, pausing there to say quietly, 'What if you are already expecting Felipe's child? Have you considered that?'

Jan steeled herself against any betraying tremor. 'I'd cope.'

'He won't let you go so easily.'

'Once I'm back in England, he won't have any choice,' she said, then added hardily, 'And if you were thinking of trying to reach him now to warn him, you're going to have difficulty. He'll still be with Sabatine.'

The suitcases were kept in a box-room at the end of the corridor. It took her only a few minutes to find her own and fling in an assortment of clothing. She would be using the money because she needed it, but everything else Felipe had given her he could keep. She wanted no reminders of this time.

Except that she had one she couldn't leave behind, of course, but she wouldn't allow that fact to deter her now. Felipe would never know.

Leda was still standing where she had left her when she went downstairs again. Her face looked pinched.

'I've told Juan he mustn't allow you to have the keys to the car,' she said. 'I'm sorry, but I can't let you go this way.'

'Then I'll send for a taxi.' Jan was moving as she spoke, lifting the telephone receiver to dial the operator with a finger that felt totally nerveless. Her request for the number of a taxi-cab company in Jerez brought her a choice of three. She dialled the first one, asked for a car to be sent out immediately to take a passenger to Seville airport, and was assured it would be with her in less than half an hour.

Felipe wouldn't be back by then, she told herself dully. He was otherwise engaged. It was quite likely he had been with Sabatine yesterday, too.

'At least be comfortable while you wait,' Leda suggested, obviously at a loss for any further persuasion. 'Come and sit down.'

Jan shook her head. 'I'll wait outside. I want to know when the taxi arrives.'

It was still only a little after noon. She took a seat on the arched veranda where she could watch the gates, her suitcase ready at her feet. Leda made no attempt to accompany her. Not that there was anything she could say or do that was going to make any difference. Right now there was little feeling. That would come later. Only it wouldn't bring her back.

She heard the telephone start ringing, but made no move. The call was hardly going to be for her, anyway.

When Leda came out to where she sat, she didn't even turn her head.

'That was the winery,' the other girl announced. She sounded odd, her voice strained. 'Felipe has been taken to the hospital.'

Jan felt her heart give a sudden sickening jolt. 'I don't believe it,' she said tonelessly.

'It's true. I would never lie to you about such a thing. He is, apparently, very ill. Blood poisoning, they believe.' Her voice took on urgency. 'Janita, he could die!'

'Not this fast,' she denied, yet the doubt was there in her mind. Blood poisoning was a serious matter. Who was she to say whether or not it could prove fatal? The question was, did she care?

The answer was blindingly obvious. Of course she did! It was caring so much that was driving her to do this—making it so impossible to reconcile herself to accepting Sabatine's place in his life. She was carrying Felipe's child. He had at least a right to know that. How could she have thought otherwise?

Coming unsteadily to her feet, she said, 'Do you know where the hospital is?'

'Of course. It's a private clinic. We can be there in twenty minutes. Juan will deal with the taxi-driver when he arrives.'

Afterwards, Jan could remember little of the journey. The clinic was a sparkling white edifice set in its own grounds on the outskirts of the town. Inside, they found the reception desk, and were told that Señor de Rimados had been taken straight into intensive care. They could go up to the floor, but no visitors were allowed as yet.

In the elevator, Jan made every effort to keep fear in check. It had only been two days since the injury. It surely took longer than that for infection to run rife through the system? Felipe was strong. Antibiotics would soon pull him through. Of course they would!

There was a smaller reception area on the second floor. The uniformed nurse at the desk invited them to take a seat and asked if they would like coffee. The doctors were still with Señor de Rimados, she said.

An age seemed to pass. Jan couldn't bring herself to touch the coffee. There was a cold dread inside her. Supposing she was too late? Supposing she never got the chance to tell Felipe about the baby? Sabatine didn't matter any more. If he lived, she would make sure he had no need of any other woman. He had to live, she thought desperately. Life without him held nothing for her.

It was Dr Valdes who finally came to them. He looked tired himself. His patient had gone into shock from a massive and virulent infection, he told them. He was stabilised at present, but still not out of danger. As in all cases of severe shock, there was the risk of kidney or even brain damage if blood pressure was not brought up to normal within a certain time.

'You may see him for five minutes, no longer,' he told Jan. 'He is still only semi-conscious, so do not be too disturbed if he has no recognition.'

Prepared as she was, the sight of the pale, clammy face on the pillow came as a shock. He was connected to a continuous blood-pressure recorder and an ECG machine, with a tube feeding whole blood into an arm. His eyes were closed, his mouth relaxed—vulnerable. She wanted to put her lips to his and feed warmth and colour into them.

The nurse in attendance left her alone with him. Jan put out a hand and touched the lean cheek, feeling the muscle contract a little beneath her fingers. His eyes opened, unfocused for a second or two, then slowly taking on intelligence. A faint smile appeared momentarily.

'I should have listened to you, *querida*,' he murmured. 'Pride already cost me dear.'

'You mustn't talk,' she said softly. 'You have to conserve your strength.'

The smile came again. 'I feel stronger already for having you here. You'll stay?'

'Of course.' There would come a time when she had to tell him the truth, but that time wasn't now. 'Wild horses wouldn't drag me away.'

He was asleep when the nurse came to tell her the five minutes were up. His colour looked a little better, Jan thought. Leda greeted her eagerly.

'How is he?'

'He'll be all right,' she said with conviction. She sat down heavily, running her fingers through her sticky hair. 'It's been quite a day!'

'Felipe doesn't have to know about it,' said Leda carefully. 'No one need know. I'll swear Juan to secrecy.'

Jan shook her head. 'I can't let it go at that. But it can wait.' She stirred herself. 'I should let them know how he is.'

'I'll do that,' Leda offered. 'There are rooms available for relatives who wish to stay on the premises. Why do you not take one and rest? You look exhausted.' She took agreement for granted. 'I'll ask the nurse to arrange it.'

The room to which Jan was shown some minutes later would have graced any first-class hotel. But then the whole place was built to high standards. There was even a bathroom adjoining, complete with separate shower and thick-piled towels. Leda came in as she finished inspecting it.

'I telephoned Gaspar, too,' she said. 'He wanted to come, but I dissuaded him.' She added, 'I think it perhaps best if I return to the house and pack a change of clothing for you. Carlos can bring it in.'

'Thanks,' Jan said gratefully. 'You're a friend in need!'

She took a shower after the other girl had gone, then got into the thick towelling robe so thoughtfully provided. What it must cost to be treated in a place such as this she hated to think, but Felipe could no doubt afford it. His son would probably be delivered here, too.

And what makes you so sure it's going to be a boy? she asked herself, lying listlessly on the bed. For herself, she didn't care, but Felipe would. She loved him; if today had shown her nothing else, it had proved that much. She believed he felt something for her, only Sabatine still held that fatal attraction. They would have to talk about it—bring it out into the open. He must be made to realise that he couldn't have them both. As to the other—well, what they had done once, they could always do again. She would want more than one child, anyway.

Her clean clothing arrived at five. Dressed in the lemon silk, with her hair caught up and back from her face with a bandeau, she felt revitalised. When they came to tell her Felipe was awake and asking for her, she went with eager steps.

He was still connected to the machines, but sitting propped up a little more this time. His colour was almost back to normal.

'They tell me you took a room,' he said. 'That's good. I want to know you're near.'

Jan sat down in the chair set ready at the bedside and took the hand he moved towards her. 'How do you feel?' she asked.

'Weak,' he admitted. 'But getting stronger by the minute. How did you discover I'd been brought here?'

'They telephoned from the winery.' She paused, only now realising what that signified. 'So you were back there when you were overcome?'

His brows drew together. 'Back?'

Too soon, she thought ruefully. 'A slip of the tongue,' she prevaricated.

His regard had sharpened. 'I don't think so. You and Leda were in Jerez this morning?'

Jan nodded unhappily. 'Yes, but it isn't important. Not right now.'

'You saw me with Sabatine,' he said as if she hadn't spoken. 'Isn't that so?'

She dropped her eyes, biting her lip. 'Yes.'

'And believed what of the meeting?'

'What else could I believe?'

His smile had a wry quality. 'The same question I asked myself when I was told of your meeting with Luis Fernández. Not the way it appeared, you told me. I make the same plea to you now, with the hope of better trust than I displayed.'

Jan looked at him long and hard. 'You're saying it wasn't arranged?'

'It was arranged, yes, but for reasons other than those which might suggest themselves.' He was silent for a moment, apparently gathering his resources, staying her with a movement of his head when she attempted to speak. 'No, we must have this straight between us. It is vital to me. Sabatine asked me to meet her because she had something important to tell me. I went because I wanted to tell her there was nothing to be gained from trying to come between us.' The hand clasping hers tightened its grip. 'To tell her I could never contemplate letting you go.'

'Even if I never gave you the one thing you want above everything else?' she asked, and saw his expression undergo a change.

'If that should happen, we will do what I would have done had all else failed, and adopt a child, but you will still be my wife. I want *nothing* more than that!'

There was no doubt left in her now, only a happiness that threatened to spill over. She had it all!

From the look in his eyes, her emotions were emblazoned on her face. 'Say it to me, Janita,' he commanded softly. 'I want to hear the words on your lips.'

'I love you,' she murmured. 'I only let myself realise it when I thought you might die. Felipe, I . . .'

He reached up a hand and slid it about her neck, drawing her down to him with a surprising strength. His kiss cherished her, sending tremor after tremor through her body.

'We shouldn't be doing this,' she whispered against his lips. 'It can't be good for you.'

'The best medicine in the world.' His voice was soft, the arrogance wiped from his face by a tenderness she had never hoped to see there. 'You changed my life, *pequeña*. Without you, I am nothing!'

Her smile was shaky. In a little while she was going to fill his cup to overflowing, but for the moment she couldn't find the words.

'You still didn't tell me what Sabatine wanted,' she said instead, and saw a faint shadow cross his face.

'You still doubt my word?'

'Not for a moment. I'm just—curious, that's all.'

He relaxed again. 'She wanted to ask me my opinion of Luis Fernández as a husband for her.'

'What did you tell her?'

'I was feeling too ill by then to make any judgement. I really don't care who she marries,' he added, dismissing the subject for all time. 'My own marriage is the only one in which I have an interest. We have a great deal to make up for, the two of us, *querida*.'

'And a long and happy life together in which to do it,' she said softly, and sent a silent prayer of thanks to the gypsy who had predicted that future.

From *New York Times* Bestselling author
Penny Jordan, a compelling novel of ruthless passion
that will mesmerize readers everywhere!

PennyJordan

Silver

Real power, true power came from
Rothwell. And Charles vowed to have it,
the earldom and all that went with it.

Silver vowed to destroy Charles, just as surely and
uncaringly as he had destroyed her father; just as he had
intended to destroy her. She needed him to want her . . .
to desire her . . . until he'd do anything to have her.

But first she needed a tutor: a man who wanted no one.
He would help her bait the trap.

**Played out on a glittering international stage,
Silver's story leads her from the luxurious comfort of
British aristocracy into the depths of adventure,
passion and danger.**

AVAILABLE IN OCTOBER!

 HARLEQUIN

Take 4 bestselling love stories FREE

Plus get a FREE surprise gift!

PASSPORT TO ROMANCE
SWEEPSTAKES RULES

1. **HOW TO ENTER:** To enter, you must be the age of majority and complete the official entry form, or print your name; address, telephone number and age on a plain piece of paper and mail to: Passport to Romance, P.O. Box 9056, Buffalo, NY 14269-9056. No mechanically reproduced entries accepted.

2. All entries must be received by the CONTEST CLOSING DATE, DECEMBER 31, 1990 TO BE ELIGIBLE.

3. **THE PRIZES:** There will be ten (10) Grand Prizes awarded, each consisting of a choice of a trip for two people from the following list:
   i)   London, England (approximate retail value $5,050 U.S.)
   ii) England, Wales and Scotland (approximate retail value $6,400 U.S.)
   iii) Carribean Cruise (approximate retail value $7,300 U.S.)
   iv) Hawaii (approximate retail value $9,550 U.S.)
   v)   Greek Island Cruise in the Mediterranean (approximate retail value $12,250 U.S.)
   vi) France (approximate retail value $7,300 U.S.)

4. Any winner may choose to receive any trip or a cash alternative prize of $5,000.00 U.S. in lieu of the trip.

5. **GENERAL RULES:** Odds of winning depend on number of entries received.

6. A random draw will be made by Nielsen Promotion Services, an independent judging organization, on January 29, 1991, in Buffalo, NY, at 11:30 a.m. from all eligible entries received on or before the Contest Closing Date.

7. Any Canadian entrants who are selected must correctly answer a time-limited, mathematical skill-testing question in order to win.

8. Full contest rules may be obtained by sending a stamped, self-addressed envelope to: "Passport to Romance Rules Request", P.O. Box 9998, Saint John, New Brunswick, Canada E2L 4N4.

9. Quebec residents may submit any litigation respecting the conduct and awarding of a prize in this contest to the Régie des loteries et courses du Québec.

10. Payment of taxes other than air and hotel taxes is the sole responsibility of the winner.

11. Void where prohibited by law.

COUPON BOOKLET OFFER TERMS

To receive your Free travel-savings coupon booklets, complete the mail-in Offer Certificate on the preceeding page, including the necessary number of proofs-of-purchase, and mail to: Passport to Romance, P.O. Box 9057, Buffalo, NY 14269-9057. The coupon booklets include savings on travel-related products such as car rentals, hotels, cruises, flowers and restaurants. Some restrictions apply. The offer is available in the United States and Canada. Requests must be postmarked by January 25, 1991. Only proofs-of-purchase from specially marked "Passport to Romance" Harlequin® or Silhouette® books will be accepted. The offer certificate must accompany your request and may not be reproduced in any manner. Offer void where prohibited or restricted by law. LIMIT FOUR COUPON BOOKLETS PER NAME, FAMILY, GROUP, ORGANIZATION OR ADDRESS. Please allow up to 8 weeks after receipt of order for shipment. Enter quickly as quantities are limited. Unfulfilled mail-in offer requests will receive free Harlequin® or Silhouette® books (not previously available in retail stores), in quantities equal to the number of proofs-of-purchase required for Levels One to Four, as applicable.

PR-SWPS

OFFICIAL SWEEPSTAKES ENTRY FORM

Complete and return this Entry Form immediately—the more Entry Forms you submit, the better your chances of winning!
- Entry Forms must be received by **December 31, 1990**
- A random draw will take place on **January 29, 1991**
- Trip must be taken by **December 31, 1991**

3-HP-1-SW

YES, I want to win a PASSPORT TO ROMANCE vacation for two! I understand the prize includes round-trip air fare, accommodation and a daily spending allowance.

Name_____

Address_____

City_____ State_____ Zip_____

Telephone Number_____ Age_____

Return entries to: **PASSPORT TO ROMANCE**, P.O. Box 9056, Buffalo, NY 14269-9056

COUPON BOOKLET/OFFER CERTIFICATE

Item	LEVEL ONE Booklet 1	LEVEL TWO Booklet 1 & 2	LEVEL THREE Booklet 1, 2 & 3	LEVEL FOUR Booklet 1, 2, 3 & 4
Booklet 1 = $100+	$100+	$100+	$100+	$100+
Booklet 2 = $200+		$200+	$200+	$200+
Booklet 3 = $300+			$300+	$300+
Booklet 4 = $400+				$400+
Approximate Total Value of Savings	$100+	$300+	$600+	$1,000+
# of Proofs of Purchase Required	4	6	12	18
Check One				

Name_____

Address_____

City_____ State_____ Zip_____

Return Offer Certificates to: **PASSPORT TO ROMANCE**, P.O. Box 9057, Buffalo, NY 14269-9057

Requests must be postmarked by **January 25, 1991**

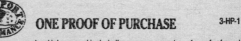

ONE PROOF OF PURCHASE

3-HP-1

To collect your free coupon booklet you must include the necessary number of proofs-of-purchase with a properly completed Offer Certificate

See previous page for details